## When things don't go the way you plan...

I was walking along the road in just-below-freezing weather, wearing running shoes, jeans, gloves, and a short-sleeved T-shirt, carrying a winter jacket with a nearly dead dog wrapped inside. Great sight.

I couldn't see any farm houses, and I had no idea where the first one would be. I started talking out loud to God.

"I sure could use some help here, Lord. I mean, I need a lot of help. But right now, if you want this dog to survive, you had better do something. I know I can't do any more. I'm likely going to get pneumonia as it is. So please, if you aren't too busy, could you help out?"...

I heard a motor behind me and turned just in time to see a brown minivan speed by. It made no attempt to stop.

People are like that sometimes. They walk right by without even seeming to notice you. I wonder if they don't care or if they're just too busy with their own thoughts.

"Thanks a lot, God," I said. Then I felt ashamed. Like it was his fault the van hadn't stopped. The person driving the van had made that choice.

I heard another motor, and I turned again. It was the tow truck from Winter's Garage, pulling a car behind it. As the truck went past, my heart sank.

**Books by N. J. Lindquist**

**Novels**

"Circle of Friends" series
***Best of Friends***
***Friends Like These***

"Growing Up and Taking Hold" series
***In Time of Trouble***

Mystery
***Shaded Light: A Manziuk and Ryan Mystery***

**Non-fiction for teens**

***The Bridge—Volume 1***
***The Bridge—Volume 2***

http://members.home.net/thats-life

*Circle of Friends series...*

# FRIENDS LIKE THESE

**N. J. Lindquist**

That's Life! Communications

Markham, Canada

**Friends Like These**



Cover design by Karen Petherick

That's Life! Communications
Box 487 Markham, ON L3P 3R1
Call tollfree 1-877-THATSLI(FE)
(in Toronto area 905-471-1447)
Email: thats-life@home.com
http://members.home.net/thats-life

Canadian Cataloguing in Publication Data

Lindquist, N.J. (Nancy J.), 1948-
Friends like these

ISBN: 0-9685495-2-7

1. Title

PS8573.I53175F74 1999 jC813'.54 C99-931771-7
PZ7.L56Fr 1999

To the main guys in my life:
Les, Kit, Mark, Daniel, and Jeffrey.

# 1

Charlie Thornton was probably the only person in our small town who didn't know I was dating Nicole Grant.

That's because Charlie spent Christmas holidays in Florida visiting his grandparents and recovering from the fight he'd had with Phil Trent in the middle of Harry's Restaurant.

Of course, I knew Charlie wouldn't stay in the dark long. But I sure didn't expect Phil, my best friend since nursery school, to be the one to bring him up to speed.

As I followed Phil out of history class on the first Monday morning after Christmas holidays, I heard him say to Charlie, "Guess you sure lost this one, eh?"

Charlie stopped dead and stared at Phil. "What are you talking about? What did I lose? Not the fight I had with you before Christmas!"

Hearing this, I tried to escape by going sideways down the hall. I didn't get far before bumping into a broken, half-open locker. No big deal, except the belt loop on the back of my jeans hooked onto the locker's catch.

"Bet you can't guess who's been dating Nicole Grant all through Christmas holidays?" teased Phil. I say "teased," but I don't mean the nice kind of teasing.

"Look," Charlie said. "If you've got something to tell me, why don't you just say it?"

They stood in the middle of the school hallway, Charlie's carefully-styled blond head more or less nose-to-nose with Phil's dark, curly one.

"We all know you've done everything possible to get a date with her," was Phil's response.

"Phil, why don't you just go to your next class? You aren't going to start another fight with me." Charlie started walking.

"Looks like she found a better man," continued Phil, a big smile on his face.

I wanted to yell, "Shut up, you idiot!" but of course I couldn't do that without drawing attention to myself—and to my being attached to a locker.

Charlie stopped and glared at Phil. "I heard you tried to date Nicole yourself."

This happened to be true, but it didn't seem to bother Phil. He grinned and said, "When you find out, you're going to feel so stupid!"

Charlie was moving again. "You're just trying to start an argument."

"Glen Sauten, that's who!" Phil's voice was triumphant. "How's that for a nice surprise?"

Several people laughed. Charlie came to a dead stop. I couldn't see his face, but I heard his voice clearly. He said, "Yeah, right, she's dating Glen. Nice try."

"No lie, buddy."

"Nicole went out with Glen," Charlie stated in a matter-of-fact voice as he turned to face Phil again. "As if!"

"No joke, man."

"Give it up. He wouldn't even have the guts to ask her."

Phil shrugged. "Maybe she asked him."

I had managed to free my belt loop from the grasp of the locker, and I was backing carefully down the hall away from them. So what if my next class was in the opposite direction?

"Sure she did," replied Charlie. "How stupid do you think I am, anyway?"

"Why don't you ask her?" challenged Phil. "Or why don't you ask how many kids have seen them together this past week?"

"Don't you ever give up?" Charlie's voice sounded more than a little annoyed.

"Why should I? It's true." Phil broke into a mocking sing-song. "Nicole likes Glen." He repeated it several times.

Marta Billing's strident voice rang out. She seemed to be gloating—as though she took great pleasure in putting Charlie in his place, which of course she did. "He's right, Charlie. Nicole and Glen have been going around together. Holding hands and all that mushy stuff."

Several voices mumbled agreement, and all of a sudden there was an explosive "What?" from Charlie, followed by a string of words starting with "that" and sounding like "creep" and "two-timer" and "dirty no-good" and "loser" and a few others I won't repeat here, and ending with my name.

Thanks a lot, Phil. I turned a corner and got out of there.

I don't know if I need to add here that Charlie and Phil don't exactly like each other. I think saying they hate each others' guts would be closer to the truth.

Well, maybe not in Charlie's case. But Phil has disliked Charlie from the day Charlie moved here. Phil had been the best football and basketball player until Charlie arrived—not to mention the top guy with the girls. But all of a sudden Phil was second best. So from day one, they were like two stags, each trying to prove himself better than the other, and getting their antlers stuck together half the time.

But what really made Phil hate Charlie's guts was just before Christmas when Phil's girlfriend, Lisa Ramsdale, had broken up with him to go out with Charlie. Since then, Phil has absolutely loathed Charlie. And Charlie seems to take pleasure in dumping on Phil whenever he gets the chance.

As for Marta—like Phil, I've known her since nursery school. She was a pain in the butt even then. Now, with her long straight black hair and her black clothes and even black lipstick, she makes me think of a Halloween ad for witch costumes. And the way she acts doesn't exactly contradict the idea. But Charlie was dating her before he asked Lisa out. Okay, he was mostly dating her to make Nicole jealous so she would date him. Oh, man, does this sound complicated!

Anyway, there I was stuck in the middle like when you play monkey in the middle with a ball and a little kid. It's okay for a while, but eventually the kid gets frustrated if you don't let him catch the ball once in a while.

Phil got upset when I was friendly to Charlie. I didn't see why Phil should tell me who I could have for a friend. But now Charlie wasn't my friend either. I had dated the girl he wanted, the girl who had totally shocked me when she said she liked me better than him.

Now I was waiting for the ball to drop—and I figured it would likely fall on my head.

I made it through the next class and part way through lunch before Charlie appeared at my side. Brett Lovansky and

Mac Robertson had been eating with me, but the rats scurried away when Charlie showed up.

Charlie had a big smile on his face as he said, "So, Glen, why don't you tell me all about it?"

I kept chewing, but my tuna sandwich turned into Styrofoam in my mouth.

"I've been hearing the strangest stories." Charlie's voice was soft, but it scared me more than it would have if he'd yelled.

I cleared my throat. I glanced around, hoping to find somebody—anybody—who could help me out. A waste of time. The cafeteria was three-quarters full of kids, but no one seemed interested in Charlie and me.

Back to reality.

Charlie lowered himself onto the chair Brett had vacated. "I'm still waiting," he said.

My dry lips managed to push out a few barely audible words. "Well, you see, Nicole—uh—she—uh—she likes me."

"So it's true? She's been going out with you?"

"Well, she went to the youth Christmas party with me and we've done things together three or four times since."

The smile left his face and he lost his friendly manner. "You?" It's hard to put on paper the disdain that word carried. If I'd been deflatable, I'd have just withered through a crack in the tile floor. His fist was waggling in my face, index finger pointing at me. "If you expect me to believe for one minute that Nicole Grant wants to go out with you, forget it!"

Aside from getting into one of those back and forth, "Yes, she does"/"No, she doesn't" arguments, I didn't know what more to say. But Charlie didn't seem to expect an answer. He stared at me for a long, uncomfortable moment, and then he leaned his elbows on the cafeteria table and stared into space. I eased off my chair and started for the door.

"Where do you think you're going?" he growled as he swung around.

I stopped and faced him. "Uh, I thought—you know—that you were finished."

"I'm finished all right! Finished letting you think you're a friend of mine! Finished pretending you're anything except a weasel who doesn't have the brains of a woodpecker! Why I was stupid enough to let you hang out with me since I moved here—! I guess I felt sorry for you. Well, I don't any more!"

In one motion, he stood up and grabbed the front of my shirt. "If I ever catch you with Nicole, you'll find out how it feels to have Charlie Thornton on your case! Got it, creep?" With that, he strode angrily out of the cafeteria.

I took a deep breath and blew the air out. Although I'd known from the first time I dated Nicole that Charlie would be angry when he found out, I really hadn't known how he would react. I could live with his threats. It was what else he might do that worried me.

I looked around. Not one single person was looking in my direction. Yeah, right. They were pretending they hadn't noticed. But by the end of the day, everybody in the school would know what had happened. They'd all be waiting to find out if I was scared of Charlie.

I gathered the remains of my half-eaten lunch and walked slowly to the recycling bins.

Weird.

I mean, weird that with all the guys in our town who had been begging her for a date, Nicole Grant should decide to like me. Me! Glen Sauten, youngest and least exciting of six Sautens, average height, average build, average looks, average brown hair, average brains–average everything.

Until Charlie moved to our town four months ago, my life had been uneventful and safe. I mean that in a good way. Since he'd moved here, a lot had happened, both good and bad. But nothing had prepared me for explaining what I had been doing going out with the only girl in town he had failed to date—and, naturally, the only one he really wanted!

I trudged to my locker, my mind spinning in circles, trying to figure out if there was anything I could do to keep the peace with Charlie. I had absolutely no desire to get into fights and stuff, and as a Christian now I didn't think I should, but I really couldn't see any way out of it if Charlie meant what he'd just said.

Charlie and I had been friends since he'd moved to our town at the beginning of the school year in September, and I thought I knew him better than anybody. Everyone else sees him as intelligent and rich and good-looking and polite. For a long time, I thought the same. I also thought he was my best friend. But just before Christmas, I came to realize he is only really concerned about Charlie Thornton.

Having him for a friend had been like being on a roller-coaster ride. Having him for an enemy was something I didn't want to think about.

But neither did I want to think about never going out with Nicole again. Besides, she'd soon hear about Charlie's threat. If I told her I didn't want to go out with her, she'd think it was because I was a coward. The whole school would. Heck, who'm I kidding? In a place the size of Wallace—population 1982 as of January first this year—the whole *town* would think I was a coward!

I made it through afternoon classes without getting yelled at more than three times. Don't ask me what the classes were about, though—I spent the whole time mulling over my options. Go out with Nicole and have Charlie for my enemy, or not go out with Nicole and have her and everybody else think I'm a coward. How about a third choice?

Way too soon, the last bell rang.

I turned to look at Charlie and knocked my pen on the floor. Nervously leaning over to pick it up, I knocked my book onto the floor on the other side. Klutz. Stupid klutz. Can't you do anything without making a fool of yourself? I finally found the pen as somebody else set my book on the desk. I looked up and saw Nicole.

She smiled. "Ready?"

I turned to look toward the back of the room. Charlie was standing there, legs apart, arms folded on his chest, watching.

The teacher left the room, but nearly everyone else pretended to be looking for a book or doing some last minute work to give them an excuse to stay.

I shut my eyes and slumped into the seat. Surely Charlie wouldn't start a fight right here!

"Glen, are you coming?" Nicole's voice seemed far away.

For a second, I wished I could dissolve into the floor. But of course, I couldn't. Slowly, I opened my eyes and looked up at her. She's so pretty. No. Beautiful. With her long golden hair and heart-shaped face, she looks like Cinderella might have after she became a princess.

"What are you doing, Glen?" she asked in a low voice. "I heard some story about Charlie's threatening you at lunch time. Did he?"

I stood up slowly. Charlie's eyes were burning a hole in my back.

"Uh, Nicole, I—uh, I—" Words escaped me. Not for the first time.

Nicole's green eyes were looking straight into mine. Those green, puzzled eyes waited for an explanation. "Glen, is anything wrong?"

I took a deep breath. Man or mouse. I grabbed her arm with my right hand and my books with my left hand. "I thought we were going for a milkshake," I said, loud enough for everyone in the room to hear. "Let's hurry up so we can get a booth."

Out in the hallway, Nicole's friend, Joyce Burgess, was waiting at the locker they shared. "Class late getting out?" Joyce asked.

"Let's hurry up so we can get a place to sit," I urged, desperate to change the subject.

But Nicole wrinkled her forehead. "Glen, everyone seems to be watching us."

"They are?" I shrugged, making my voice casual. "I guess I didn't notice."

"Glen? What's going on? I heard something about Charlie threatening you at lunch time. You don't really think he would do anything, do you? He has absolutely nothing to say about who I date. I'll talk to him if you want." She turned.

I grabbed her arm. "No. Don't say anything!"

She gave me a funny look. "Glen, you're not afraid of him are you? I know he had a fight with Phil before Christmas. But that was over Lisa. And anyway, Phil started it. You would never start a fight, would you?"

"No. No, I wouldn't."

"I hope not." She didn't look convinced.

"Well, are we going for a Coke or not?"

A hand clapped me on the back. "Way to go, buddy!"

Phil. Just what I needed.

"Get lost," I mumbled out of the side of my mouth, but either he didn't hear or he was ignoring me.

"Way to go!" he repeated.

Nicole and Joyce both stared at him.

"Thanks a lot," I muttered.

"Going to Harry's?"

"Yeah."

"Let's go then. We can talk on the way."

Remembering it was cold outside, I grabbed my winter jacket from my locker. There was a book I should have looked for too, but this was not the time to worry about mundane things like homework.

The four of us left the school and started toward Harry's Restaurant. It took us about ten minutes to get to Main Street, where all but a few stores are located.

I didn't say much as we walked. Neither did Phil. I wanted to ask him what he thought he was doing, butting in like he was, but I couldn't very well. I wanted to tell him not to talk about Charlie and his threat, but I couldn't do that, either. I did make a face at him once. He asked me if I had something in my eye, and then Nicole and Joyce wanted to know if I was okay. I gave up.

Harry's Restaurant has been the main hangout for kids in Wallace for 40 years. According to my oldest sister, the decor hasn't changed in all that time. There's a long brown and beige counter with a dozen red stools in front of the kitchen area, and there are four tables with chairs between the counter and the outside windows. Then along one side, going back into a corner next to the enclosed part of the kitchen, there are six booths with high-backed red plastic seats and brown melamine tabletops. The walls are beige with posters of sports cars, and the curtains on the windows that line the front wall are red with brown and beige polka dots.

Some other kids were already there, but I didn't see Charlie, so I relaxed. We sat in a booth in the back corner and drank milkshakes and ate French fries and talked about ordinary stuff. Actually, Nicole and Joyce did most of the talking. I never have had a lot to say, and besides, I still felt like I should be pinching myself to find out if this was real.

Phil was a lot quieter than usual. He spent most of his time looking around, like he was watching for somebody.

Maybe Lisa. He'd dated her all last summer and fall before they quarreled and she went out with Charlie.

Phil left us outside the restaurant. Joyce lives on a farm twenty minutes from town, but her mom was in town today to do some shopping and was going to pick her up at the Grants' later, so the three of us walked to Nicole's house.

We were talking about school starting and other mundane things when Nicole suddenly said, "You're going to be working hard the rest of the year, aren't you Glen?"

"Working" and "hard" are not words I normally use. "Huh?"

"Schoolwork. You know you need good marks to get into college. Your marks haven't always been the greatest. You are going to be studying hard, aren't you? I know you could get better marks if you just put in more effort."

I hadn't thought much about it. Studying and I aren't exactly on a first name basis. "I guess." I shrugged.

"I'll help you if you want."

The thought of studying with Nicole sure beat the thought of not studying by myself. "That'd be great," I said with a lot more enthusiasm.

"But you'll really have to work." She laughed, her eyes sparkling up at me.

"Rats."

We came to her house. "Well, thanks for the milkshake, Glen," she said.

Joyce said, "Yes, Glen, thanks. You know you didn't have to pay for mine."

"Uh, that's okay." I looked at the sidewalk. "Dad and Mom wouldn't let me buy the car I wanted, so I've got all this money I saved from my job last summer just sitting in my bank account gathering interest."

"Well, don't spend all your money on us," Nicole said. "You'll need it for college."

For one brief instant she sounded just like my dad. I stared at her.

"You have applied, haven't you?"

"I—uh. Oh—oh, yeah, sure."

Then Joyce opened the door and Nicole started to follow her inside.

"Nicole?"

She turned. "Yes, Glen?"

"I just wondered—well, with school in and everything, it's harder to see you. Should we figure out what we want to do? I mean, like, do you want to do something Friday? Maybe go bowling?" We have a small bowling alley in town. Actually, it's beside Ed's Pool Hall and Ed owns both. I wasn't sure if she would go there. Because Nicole's dad is a pastor, and because she is a Christian, she doesn't do a lot of things other kids take for granted. I was still learning what was okay with her and what wasn't.

But she immediately said, "Yes, I like bowling."

"Great."

She smiled. "I'll check with my parents and let you know for sure tomorrow. But I think it will be okay. Would it be all right if I ask Joyce to come?"

Not exactly what I had in mind. "Uh, yeah, sure. Should I get somebody else? Mac or Brett, maybe?"

"I'll ask her. She might like to invite Ted or Andy."

"Sure." I didn't really want Joyce along, and certainly not Ted or Andy or one of the other guys from the church, because I figured they were all annoyed with me for dating Nicole. Mac and Brett are easy-going buddies of mine and would be nice and safe.

"Bye." She gave me a huge smile and went inside.

That smile made me forget all about Joyce, Charlie, school, everything.

I had walked a block and a half when Charlie's car drove up beside me.

He had the passenger's window down and he leaned over to yell, "Get in!"

I ignored him and kept walking.

His car stayed beside me. "I said get in, punk!"

"I don't need a ride, thanks," I answered, trying to keep my voice normal.

We came to the end of the block and Charlie's tires squealed as he pulled his car directly across my path. Feeling a surge of adrenaline, I whipped around behind his car and tore down the next block. I cut across the elementary school grounds onto a walking path between some houses and sneaked through another walkway and a couple of backyards to the street I lived on.

Charlie couldn't follow me, because after the elementary school, which is next to the high school, the houses are built in courts and circles instead of the square blocks the rest of the town is built in. Why new areas are like that, I don't know. Usually I find it annoying. But right now I was glad. Charlie had to drive the long way around while I could cut through.

But that didn't mean he couldn't be ahead of me. And since his house is almost across the street from mine, I still had to pass by his place to get home.

Sure enough. His car was in the driveway and he was standing at the edge of the road watching for me.

I slowed to a crawl and tried to think of some way to get to my house without having to confront him.

"You look like you've been running for your life," Charlie called out when he saw me. "Did something scare you? Your shadow, maybe?"

I didn't say anything. Even if I wasn't out of breath, I wouldn't know what to say. I kept walking until I was level with his house. At the same time, Charlie crossed over to my side and stood directly in front of me.

I stopped a few feet from him.

"I told you to stay away from Nicole," he said in a menacing tone.

I stopped. "Since when do I have to do what you say?"

The words were mine, but I couldn't believe I'd had the guts to say them.

"You don't *have* to do anything," he said evenly. "But if you're smart—"

Don't ask me what would have happened next. All I know is that Mrs. Pearson, who lives three doors down from us and is at least 75 years old, came out onto her front porch just then and called out, "Glen! Glen Sauten, is that you?"

"Uh, yeah!" I tried not to look and sound too happy, but, believe me, I was happy. "Yeah, it's me! Do you need me?"

"Oh, Glen, I thought it was you I saw out there. I'm so glad you're outside. Your friend, too. I wonder if you boys would be so kind as to come and move something for me?

I've been wondering all day how to move it, but two big strong boys like you should have no trouble at all."

With a glare at me and, I suspect, another one at Mrs. Pearson, Charlie followed me into her house. It's hard to explain, but her house is a lot older than ours. It was once a farmhouse, and when they built the new subdivision, she refused to move or sell out, so they planned the lots around her house. So here she sits in her old two-story surrounded by new bungalows and split-levels.

Charlie and I pulled out a solid oak bureau for her. Apparently when she'd been dusting that morning one of the many pictures of her children and grandchildren had fallen behind, and there was no way on earth she could get it out.

She held it now, lovingly wiping it off with her apron, a smile covering her face. "Oh, thank you so much boys! I'm sure I don't know how I'd have managed without you. Come and have some juice and cookies."

I quickly accepted her offer. Charlie said he had to go. He glared at me before he left. But I was feeling pretty good. Fate seemed to be on my side this time.

## 2

I came out of my euphoria with a thud when I opened my school books after dinner and remembered what Nicole had said about my needing to work hard. She'd even offered to help me. But while Nicole is one of the best students in our school, I knew I couldn't depend on her to get me through. I was going to have to really get down and work. Not because of college, since I wasn't at all sure I wanted to go there, but because I didn't want Nicole to think I was dumb.

Was she worth it?

Stupid question!

So I was going to have to work hard.

And I was also going to have to watch how I acted. We'd only been dating two weeks, so in a way we were still getting to know each other. I mean, beyond the way you know somebody you've gone to school with. The last thing I wanted was for her to start thinking I was stupid.

Most people do think that. I mean they just don't expect a lot from me. To be honest, I've never given them any reason to think differently.

I picked up the math text. Just before Christmas, Dad had helped me with some stuff I didn't understand. He'd done a good job, too. I understood that section fairly well now. I'd have to get him to help me more often.

I put the math book down and picked up my history text. After reading a few pages, I groaned. This wasn't going to be fun.

And then I remembered something. God was supposed to be helping me now. I mean, I'd asked his Son, Jesus, to come into my life and take over, so presumably he had. Pastor Grant, Nicole's dad, had said I could make God unhappy by not letting him do anything, or I could please him by asking him to help me do what was right. I had a feeling studying and getting decent grades would be something God considered right to do. So maybe he'd help.

"God," I whispered, "if you're really here inside me like Pastor Grant said, I pray that you'll help me. You know I haven't been much at working in school. I've been happy if I scraped through. I know you won't just give me the marks—I have to do the work—but it's not going to be easy. I'll need a lot of help just to get going. I sure hope you'll be with me.

"I hope you'll help me with Charlie, too. I know he hates me, and I guess I don't blame him, but I'm not sure what to do when he threatens me and stuff like that. I don't think Christians go around fighting all the time, and anyway, if I fought Charlie, I'm sure he'd win. But what would that prove? I'm not going to stop dating Nicole just because he beats me up. I don't think that would get her too excited about him, either. He's nuts! Anyway, I pray you'll help me know what to say to him."

After that, I felt better. But I still had to open the history book and start reading. I sank down on my bed, book in hand.

When I woke up an hour later, I realized I'd lasted maybe ten minutes. So much for lying on the bed to read.

"Glen, telephone!" Mom called.

Thankful for an excuse not to study, I went to the phone.

Phil's voice asked, "So, how do you like going around with Nicole?"

"Uh, fine."

"Just 'fine'?"

"Well, what do you think?"

There was silence on the other end. I figured I knew what was going through Phil's mind. Until Charlie showed up last fall, Phil was the most popular guy in our school. Don't get me wrong, they aren't much alike. As I said before, Charlie is fair-skinned with blond hair while Phil is dark—almost swarthy and looks a bit like a motorcycle gang member. Charlie is always smiling; Phil tends to look sullen. Charlie dresses in the latest clothes and always looks like someone on a magazine cover; Phil wears torn jeans and faded T-shirts. But they have two things in common: one is that they are both good at sports; the other is that all the girls like them.

Except Nicole. Phil had given up trying to get her to date him long before Charlie showed up last fall, but that didn't mean her refusal didn't still irritate him. Of course, he would have been even more irritated had it been Charlie she was dating. With me—well, like Charlie, he was no doubt having a hard time just believing it was true.

"Phil?" I said.

"Just thinking. You got any idea what Charlie will do?"

"Clobber me the first chance he gets." I told him what had happened on the way home from Nicole's.

"I expected him to follow you to Harry's. Why do you think I went there with you? Or did you think I wanted to tag along with you and Nicole? Then I decided he'd wait till you were alone. But I never thought he'd wait around until after you dropped off Joyce and Nicole."

"Well, it worked out okay."

"So far."

"You think getting even with me by hitting me is on top of his priority list?"

Phil laughed. "You'll be lucky if all he does is hit you."

"You sound pleased by the idea."

"Well, I'm not sure I don't resent the fact that you of all people has made it with Nicole. I mean—come on, Glen, even you have to admit how unlikely it is."

"That's nice to hear from my so-called best friend."

Phil refused the bait. "What are you going to do about Charlie?" he asked.

"Stay out of his way, I guess."

"How the heck are you going to do that? As you just reminded me, you live across the street from him."

"How should I know?" I felt irritated, not so much by Phil's question as by my own inability to take care of the situation. "I don't know what I'm going to do, Phil," I said morosely. "I don't really think there's anything much I can do. If he wants to beat me up, I guess he will. Anyway, I prayed about it and I figure it's up to God to look after me now."

As usual, Phil ignored the God stuff. "You could learn to fight."

"I can't even play dodgeball without tripping over my own feet! And he's about 50 pounds heavier than me. All muscle."

"You could have your dad talk to his dad." Phil's voice wavered slightly.

"Yeah—" I tried to sound sarcastic "—or I could get my mom to talk to his mom."

"You could have Nicole ask him to leave you alone." Phil's voice was close to breaking up with laughter. "Or maybe she could beat him up for you."

If we'd been talking about somebody else, I might have found it as funny as he did. But we were talking about my life here, and I didn't find it funny at all. "Thanks for the help, Phil. Anything else you want before I hang up?"

"Okay, I'll be serious. Actually, I have it all figured out, Glen. What you need is a bodyguard."

"Right," I agreed. "I'll check the yellow pages under B."

"No, I'm serious, Glen. Think about it. Who is the one person in town who has never been fooled by Charlie? Me! And who is the one person who isn't afraid of him? Me! And who is the one person who's beaten Charlie in a fight? Me! So who's the best person to protect you from Charlie? It's obvious, isn't it?"

"Phil, at best it was a tie when you fought Charlie over Lisa. Even if it made sense, it wouldn't work. You can't be here all the time, as if you were my shadow."

"No, no, listen. I've got it all figured out."

I sighed.

"Charlie isn't going to beat you up when Nicole is around. He isn't stupid."

I wanted to add that not only is he not stupid, but he's smarter than Phil and I put together. Charlie is a lot of things, but dumb isn't one of them. He might even be smarter than Phil and Brett and Mac and I put together.

"Glen, are you listening?" came Phil's voice over the receiver.

"Yeah."

"What we have to watch for is when Nicole isn't around and you're alone. So we make sure you aren't alone. I pick you up in the morning and drive you home after school. At school, we make sure Charlie doesn't get an opportunity to start something. Brett and Mac can help there. One of them can be around to call me if necessary."

"What about when you're playing basketball?"

"Charlie's on the team, too, bacon brain." Right. Charlie had taken Phil's spot as center, not to mention been elected captain.

"It might work," I said reluctantly. Not that I wanted somebody else to fight Charlie for me, but if somebody was with me all the time, maybe Charlie would ignore me. It sure beat relying on Mrs. Pearson to show up.

"The trick is not to let Charlie lure you outside when I'm not around. But your mom and dad are usually home in the evenings, aren't they?"

"Yeah."

"Have them screen your calls and don't take any from Charlie. Or, if you do talk to him, just say 'no' to anything he says. Don't let him get you mad enough to do something stupid."

I wanted to argue that so far it had always been Phil who got mad at Charlie and ended up doing something stupid, but I held my tongue. After all, Phil really was trying to help me out here. "How long do you plan to keep this up?"

"Charlie's going to college in the fall, isn't he? So he can be a doctor like his old man? So, the longest it would be is until then. But I figure he'll forget all about you in a month or two. Or else, well, you know—"

"I know what?"

"Well, you know." Phil sounded uncomfortable.

"What are you talking about?"

"Well, you and Nicole. You don't need to get mad. Even *you* have to admit it's a bit hard to believe."

"Are you trying to say that she'll probably get tired of me soon, so it won't matter any more?"

"Well, she isn't exactly your type, is she?"

"She's the first girl I've dated! I don't have a type!"

"Take it easy, Glen. I think it's great you're going with Nicole. I hope she's crazy about you and she ends up marrying you, if that's what you want."

"Thanks a lot." I think I managed to get the sarcasm over the phone line.

"So it's all worked out. I'll pick you up for school in the morning and we'll go from there. Anything on this weekend?"

"Nicole and I are going bowling Friday."

"Bowling?"

"Yeah."

"You're taking Nicole Grant bowling?" He said it like I was taking her to the town dump.

"In case you've forgotten, there aren't a whole lot of choices in this town. She doesn't go to many movies, and she doesn't go to dances, so where do you expect me to take her?"

"She wants to go?"

"No, I'm making it all up!" Even studying would be better than this dopey conversation. Speaking of that, I ought to hit those books again.

"Don't lose your cool. What about Friday? You'll be with Nicole. Won't you have a car?"

"No. Mom and Dad are going to Stanton. I was going to walk over to her house and then we'd walk to the bowling alley."

"So I guess I'll drive you to the Grants'. Or should I go bowling with you and Nicole?"

I remembered that Joyce was coming, too, and that she needed a date. In spite of his strange sense of humor, I would far rather have Phil around than any other guy I know. "Come with us. Joyce is going to be there, too."

"Oh, that's a big attraction."

"She's okay."

"You owe me one, buddy. Big time."

"Yeah, but I really don't know if this makes any sense. I mean what's the worst Charlie could do?"

Phil laughed. "You don't want to know."

I sighed. Things were really getting out of hand. "I'd better go now. I should be studying."

"Yeah, since when?"

"Since now."

"Yeah." Phil laughed harder. "I guess you'd better. Otherwise Nicole will find out she's dating someone who doesn't know a noun from a fraction."

I hung up.

I wandered into the living room where Mom and Dad were watching TV and reading the newspaper. I sat in an easy chair and watched the end of the show that was on, but I couldn't even tell you what it was about. I had used studying as an excuse to end the conversation with Phil, but the reality was that at best I'm a C student. Charlie and Nicole are both straight As. I did get an A in a physics test just before the Christmas break—because for the first time in my life I really studied.

But it was one thing to work hard for one test; it was something else again to work hard all the time. I didn't even know if I could. But if it made Nicole happy....

"Dad," I said as the show ended.

"Hmm?" He didn't look up from the newspaper.

"Would you help me study math?"

That got his attention. "Right now?"

"Whenever you want."

He put the newspaper down and looked at me in what I can only describe as surprise. "Go get your books and bring them to the kitchen table," he said after a second.

So we worked on math until ten o'clock. One good thing about doing it with Dad was that I had to concentrate so hard I didn't have time to think about anything else. And when I went to bed I was so exhausted from all that thinking that I fell asleep right away.

True to his word, Phil picked me up in his car the next morning. I say "car" rather loosely. Phil's Goose—long story, but that's his name for his car—is kind of unique. That's because Phil does all the work on it himself. It's a '76 Chevy, painted mallard green, and the motor makes a good deal of noise. But it can hold it's own pretty good. He's really proud of it.

"So, are you bleary-eyed from studying?" he asked as I got in.

"Not exactly."

"Yeah? Up all night worrying, then?"

I glared at him. "No."

"Always this touchy in the morning?"

"Just drive the car. And don't forget this was your idea."

"I thought it was a good idea."

"Maybe it is."

"Why are you so grumpy then?"

"Maybe I should just let him beat me up and get it over with."

"Do you think that would impress Nicole? Black eyes, bloody nose, swollen mouth, missing teeth... Would she feel sorry for you or think you're a wimp?"

"I *am* a wimp. Why shouldn't she know it?"

Classes went okay, I guess. No worse than usual. The teachers were piling on new work.

As classes ended for lunch, Mac started toward me and then melted away when Nicole came to ask me if I'd like to go to the library and work on our English assignment.

I'd have gone to the gym and stood on my head for the whole lunch hour if Nicole had asked me to—and if I could stand on my head, which I've never been able to do. So we ate lunch quickly and then went to the library, where Nicole began to ask me questions about Shakespeare's play, *Hamlet*, which we were supposed to have read before the holidays.

"Glen, even you ought to be able to figure out when the climax is," she said at last.

"Uh, yeah," I replied.

"Okay," she said, "what about the characters? What did you think of Horatio, for instance? Was he a good friend?"

"Yeah," I said. Fifty-fifty chance of being right.

"Why?"

I floundered.

We continued like that for several more questions. When she'd had enough, she shut the book and looked at me. Her green eyes were intense. I lowered my eyes and stared at the table.

"Glen," she said evenly, "have you read the play?"

There was no point in lying to her, but I didn't want her to decide I wasn't worth her time, either. So I just sat there, silently staring at the top of the wooden table. It was maple-colored and old and beat-up from all the kids who had sat there over the years studying or avoiding studying.

"Glen, I asked you a question."

I absently tapped on the table. Her hand reached over and covered mine. "Glen, look at me," she said.

I looked up.

"Have you read the play?"

I shook my head.

"Have you read any of the books for English this year?"

I cleared my throat. "Some," I said. "When my arm was broken in the fall, I read some. I couldn't do much but read."

"Glen! How can you?"

"I'm lazy?" I hoped she would accept that.

She sighed. "I knew you didn't work very hard, but I never suspected it was this bad."

I squirmed. Was this the end?

"Well, that settles one thing," Nicole said as she began gathering up her books.

"It does?"

"Yes," she said. "I'm not going bowling with you Friday night.

"You're not?" My voice croaked. Charlie had won without a single punch. All because of my own stupidity.

"Not unless you have the play read by then. And any other assignments caught up." She smiled. "Don't look so glum. I'll help you."

I started breathing again. She still liked me! It was just that, as I'd expected, she wanted me to get good marks. So I'd have to work hard. I'd just have to!

"I'll leave you to get started reading," she said.

Before I could react, she was gone, slipping silently between chairs and tables, her long golden hair flowing behind her, just like Cinderella's probably did when she was running down the castle stairs while the clock was striking midnight.

And although I was better suited for court jester than Prince Charming, it was Prince Charming I yearned to be.

I sighed, picked up *Hamlet*, and began to read. This was going to be a long week.

When I got up to go, I discovered Mac beside me.

"Phil told me to stay with you, but if Nicole showed up, to keep my distance."

"And if Charlie shows up?"

"Well, to protect you, I guess."

Mac is a nice guy. One of my best friends. He's okay-looking if you like reddish-blond hair and a ton of freckles. But he's not much more than five and a half feet tall and I doubt if he weighs more than 100 pounds.

"Or else I could run and find Phil," he added.

I shook my head.

When I reached the hall after last class, Nicole was waiting for me. Phil was somewhere behind me.

"Did you want to go for a Coke?" I asked hopefully.

"How far did you read?"

"Uh, I think I read most of the first act. It's pretty weird."

"Not once you understand the language and what's happening. Would you like me to go over it with you?"

"Would you?"

"Of course." She smiled. "Why don't you come home with me right now so we don't waste any time?"

On the way to my locker, I grabbed Phil and told him not to worry about me because I'd be with Nicole. So I walked her home, and on the way she told me a bunch of stuff about Shakespeare and why he was such a great writer. I can't honestly say any of it sank in, especially after Charlie passed us in his car and I saw the look on his face.

Since there was really nothing I could do, I tried to put him out of my mind and concentrate on what Nicole was saying.

I'd like to say the next two hours were all fun and games, but the truth is Nicole made me work the entire time. And I mean work! Just reading the lines wasn't enough; I had to actually understand them!

At twenty to six, she said she had to set the table and I should be getting home. As I was leaving, she reminded me of some math homework we had for the next day.

I walked slowly down the sidewalk. My brain had ceased to function. It just wasn't used to this sort of thing. For a few minutes I even wondered what I'd gotten myself into. Then I reasoned that Nicole was doing all this for me, so I shouldn't be so unthankful.

A horn honked and I looked up, startled, to see Phil's car beside me.

"Going my way?" he asked as I opened the passenger door.

"Have you been sitting waiting for me the whole time?" I asked in amazement.

"More or less. And I wasn't the only one."

"Huh? You mean Charlie was here?"

"Yeah, he followed you here and parked down the street where he could watch. When you came out, he started to follow. But he saw me and kept going. I don't think he was too happy."

I sank into the seat. "Oh, man. I'm dead."

"Not yet," Phil said cheerfully.

Charlie was standing in his driveway when Phil dropped me off, but all he did was glare as Phil drove away and I went inside. I shut the door and breathed a long sigh of relief. I knew this couldn't go on, but maybe soon God would show me how to get Charlie off my back.

Mom was finishing up dinner.

I should say here that I have great parents. They've had five other kids to practice on, so they don't make many dumb mistakes. I know they love me. Dad is a bank manager, and Mom is—well—a mom. She's usually at home baking and stuff. Okay, so picture *Leave it to Beaver*, and you pretty well have my folks. With me as the Beaver, I guess.

I braced for the flood of questions I knew Mom would ask about where I'd been and what I'd been doing, but she didn't say a word. Just asked me to set the table and then ignored me. Now that I thought about it, I realized she had seemed preoccupied the day before, too. She hadn't asked me about school or about how Charlie's holidays in Florida had gone, or anything. Weird. I wondered if something was wrong.

Dad came in, and we started eating dinner. Everything was going fine when Mom suddenly said, "Matt, I've been thinking."

Something in her tone of voice made Dad and I instinctively look at each other.

"What about, Susanne?" Dad asked calmly.

"Something Carrie said when they were here for Christmas struck a chord. She was telling me about Ken's mother. Apparently, when Ken's younger sister left home, his mother went to pieces. All three of her children were away from home and she didn't know what to do with herself. She felt empty and she had too much time on her hands. She ended up getting depressed and having to see several doctors. I guess she was in a state."

"Did she get better?" Dad asked.

"Eventually. She started going out with friends, and then she discovered a program where people go into nursery schools and kindergartens to read to the kids and help those who are having difficulty learning. It's called the Grandparents' Program. She's really enjoying it.

"That's good," Dad said cautiously, as if wondering what would come next. I was wondering, too.

Mom got the rice pudding she'd made and dished it out. She didn't say anything else.

"Is that all?" I asked when the silence got to be too much.

# 3

"Is what 'all'?" Mom sounded annoyed.

"Ken's mom. Is that all you were going to say?"

"What else should I say?"

Now I knew for sure she was annoyed. I grabbed my spoon and concentrated on the pudding.

To my relief, Dad filled the gap. "I think Glen was wondering if you were comparing Ken's mother's experiences with us. Glen is a senior. When he goes to college next year, it will be the first time in almost twenty-eight years that we won't have a child to care for."

"Maybe I was thinking about that," Mom said. She didn't sound very friendly.

But I was stuck on what Dad had said. There he was again, assuming I'd be going to college! That was more than I was ready to say. First, my marks weren't good enough, and second, I had no idea what I wanted to be. But Dad had it all figured out!

Mom wasn't thinking about me. Or rather, she was, but she was considering life without me. I guess it would be a lot different with just Dad and her at home. Nobody to yell at, nobody to keep her up late waiting for him to get in, no teachers' complaints to deal with, no teenagers hanging around or phoning at all hours, and no messes to clean up. Dull.

I realized that my parents were still talking.

Dad was saying, "You know you can if you want, Susanne."

"I've never really thought about it before. I've always been involved with so many things, and the last few years, with just Glen at home, it's been great not to have to be always rushing around."

"But you do need something else," Dad said. "I know you could manage."

"But I've no experience, Matt. What would I do?"

"You've never had a job, Mom?" I asked in disbelief.

She shook her head. "Not really. I went to university for two years, and then we got married, and I finished the third year a few months before Carrie was born and—well, I didn't want to work with a new baby, and your dad had a good job."

"And Jordan came along less than a year after Carrie, and a year later there was Bruce—" added Dad.

"And then two years until Jeanne, and a year till Janice, and then five years before you decided to put in an appearance, Glen," Mom finished.

She put her elbows on the table and leaned her chin on her hands. "I never had a minute to think about doing anything else until a few years ago. And then I just thought how nice it was to have some time to do all the things I hadn't had time for before—taking painting classes and trying out new recipes and going out with friends.... It was great to have a break from all the work of raising six kids. And just let me hear somebody dare to say I haven't worked—"

"You know I didn't mean that, Mom. But you've never had a paying job?"

"Only for a couple of summers working as a clerk in a drug store when I was a teenager. I can't say I enjoyed that."

"What did you take at university?" I asked. I'd never really thought much about what my parents were like when they were young.

"Just a general arts degree." She sighed. "I'm not really trained for anything."

"Would you like to work at the bank?" Dad asked.

"No, dear. Thank you, but I'd like to do something—oh, involving people. I'll have to think about it. The real question is, would you mind if I did find a job?"

"Of course not," Dad said.

"How about you, Glen? Would you mind?"

"Er, uh, no. Whatever you want." I had to say the words, but I wasn't too happy about it. I kind of liked my home the way it was.

"Thanks, Glen. I may not find anything, but—well, I have a 50th birthday coming up in a few months. If I'm going to find a new interest, I'll have to do it before I'm too old."

"You'll never be too old for me, Susanne," Dad said.

It's amazing how he always says the right thing. Anyway, I figured it was my cue, so I ducked out fast and went to my room to do my homework.

The next morning Phil arrived early to pick me up. He seemed to be enjoying himself, but all I could think was that we were only delaying things.

I tried to pay attention in class. And I let Nicole help me again after school. We worked some more on English, and then started on history. I think I tried her patience a lot on that, but she didn't let it show—not much, anyway.

Before I left her house, I called Phil. We had decided it made more sense for me to call than for him to wait outside in the middle of winter. Fortunately, Nicole was clearing away her books and didn't ask any questions.

Every day that week, I worked, whether with Nicole or alone. My head felt it was going to burst from all the unaccustomed effort.

And for the rest of the week, nothing happened with Charlie. He just plain ignored both Nicole and me. I thought it was because I was never alone for two minutes, but Phil said he thought it was because Charlie wanted to give Nicole time to get to know me well enough so she'd dump me herself. Phil is such a good friend.

When I told Nicole and Joyce that I'd invited Phil to go bowling with us, Nicole sounded a little miffed. She said I should have asked Joyce first. Fortunately, Joyce said it was okay. But neither one seemed thrilled. Well, Phil hadn't been thrilled, either.

Neither Mom nor Dad commented on how much school work I was doing. I caught a few puzzled looks, but Mom was busy thinking about finding a job, and Dad was thinking about her, so I escaped the questions and enthusiasm they normally would have had.

What was irritating was that Charlie and everybody else had no idea how my week actually went. All they saw was me walking Nicole home every day after school and staying there until dinner. Which meant Charlie was probably getting madder and madder even though all we were actually doing was working on helping me understand that stupid play and get my homework caught up!

I wasn't really surprised when I got a call from Charlie about 6:55 Friday night. As soon as I picked up the receiver, I wished I had let Mom answer the phone. But then she'd have just called me, so it didn't really matter.

"So, Glen, buddy—"

"What do you want?"

"What's that supposed to mean?"

"You know what it means. What do you want?"

"Glen, I'm surprised. First you steal my girl; then you act like I have a contagious disease or something. Is that any way to treat a friend?"

"She never was your girl. And you don't know how to be a friend."

"You sure disappoint me, Glen. I thought I knew you."

"What was that you said again? If I went near Nicole, I'd regret it?"

"So what am I going to do? I was just surprised, that's all. I really thought she was just using you to make me jealous. If that isn't the case, then I'll back off."

"Charlie, what do you want?"

"Maybe I want my best friend Glen back."

"Maybe you want Nicole."

His voice was soft. "Oh, I'm not worried about Nicole."

"No?"

"No. When I want her, I can get her just like that." I heard a noise which presumably was his fingers snapping.

"Yeah, right," I said.

"Now, what I really don't like—" Charlie's voice became low and confiding "—is all this business with Phil. Every time I see you, there he is. Why on earth do you think you need to be afraid of me? What could I do?"

He paused, but I didn't say anything.

"Glen?"

"What?"

"You haven't answered me."

"Sorry, Charlie. I have to go. Nicole and I have a date."

The line went dead.

Phil picked me up a few minutes later.

"Charlie just called," I told him as I got into the front seat. "He asked why I needed you around to protect me."

"Yeah? He doesn't like it, huh? What's he going to do?"

"He didn't say much. But he sounded kind of—well, scary."

"Ignore him. He's all talk. And he's just plain stupid if he thinks you're going to jump whenever he says. How dumb does he think you are, anyway?"

"I expect he just thinks I'm a coward. Which I guess I am."

"Yeah? We'll show him how much of a coward you are."

"We will?"

He picked Nicole up first. It seemed funny, me sitting in back with her and Phil driving. I guess there's a first time for everything, but any other time I'd been with Phil and a girl, the girl was with him.

It was an awkward drive to where Joyce lives. For the first few minutes after we picked up Nicole, nobody said a word. I guess Phil and I were both thinking about Charlie and how mad this evening would make him.

Finally, Nicole said, "It was nice of you to come with us, Phil. And to drive."

"No problem," he said. I caught his eye in the mirror and knew he was laughing. Me and my bodyguard.

"My parents needed our car," I blurted out.

"Oh?" Nicole said.

"Yeah. They were going over to Stanton. To see some friends."

"That's nice," Nicole said.

I caught Phil's eyes in the mirror again. Actually, what I saw was Phil rolling his eyes. But for the life of me, I couldn't think of anything to say to her. Not in front of Phil. He's gone out with lots of girls, and he never has trouble talking to them. Actually, come to think of it, the girls do most of the talking and he just nods and grunts. But Nicole never talks about dumb stuff like other girls.

I for one was really glad when we arrived at Joyce's house. Or rather farm. Her dad has a dairy cow operation that's very interesting. It's all computerized. He can tell you how much milk each cow gives each time it's milked, and how much it eats, and what happens if the food has different ingredients or vitamins, and everything. It's kind of neat.

I went there with my dad one day last spring when he drove out to talk to Joyce's dad about a loan he wanted so he could add more high tech stuff. Mr. Burgess showed us all over, and we were both impressed.

Anyway, to make a long story short, we never made it back to town because I started telling Phil about the computerized cows, and Joyce offered to show us around. The next thing we knew it was an hour and a half later and we didn't feel like going bowling. So we went into the house and Joyce made popcorn and found some root beer and we played Monopoly until after eleven.

Phil and I used to play Monopoly and other games like that when we were younger, but we haven't lately. It was okay, though. In fact, it was fun. Even Phil seemed to enjoy playing, especially when one of us landed on Boardwalk or Park Place and had to pay him rent. All in all, it was an okay evening. I didn't have to talk much, except about the game, which even I could handle.

On the way home, though, we lapsed into that awkward silence again. Having Joyce around seemed to make a difference.

When the silence became more than I could take, I started bugging Phil because he'd won, but only after a few doubtful plays. Not to say he was cheating, but he came as close as you could. I, on the other hand, was the first to declare bankruptcy.

"You should never have traded North Carolina to Phil," Nicole said when I complained about my rotten luck. "Once he had that whole side sewn up, nobody could beat him."

"I guess I wasn't thinking," I explained.

"No comment," Phil said.

There was silence again for several minutes.

Then Nicole said, "Glen, I haven't seen you with Charlie this week. I hope you aren't still upset with him because he spent so much time and energy trying to get me to date him last fall. I mean, I don't want you to stop being friends because of me."

I looked at her, my mind working hard to catch up. Was I imagining it, or was Nicole sort of baiting Phil? I mean, asking me if Charlie and I were still friends in front of Phil was kind of—kind of dangerous. She must have known Phil and Charlie didn't get along. Or had she forgotten? I mumbled, "We still see each other now and then," and then felt dumb. It wasn't exactly a lie. We had five classes together at school, so we couldn't help seeing each other! But—that wasn't exactly what Nicole meant.

"So you haven't told Nicole about Charlie's threats?" said that intrusive voice from the front seat. I wanted to kill him.

"What threats?" Nicole asked. "Do you mean whatever he said in the cafeteria Monday?"

I tried to cover up. "Ignore him. It's nothing. He's talking about nothing."

But Nicole wasn't satisfied. "Phil, are you implying that Charlie has threatened Glen more than that one time?"

"Why would he imply something like that?" I asked, still trying.

"It's true Charlie was trying to date me from September on. He was getting pretty annoying. But then he started dating Lisa. He hasn't asked me out lately." She looked at me. "Is he angry with you because I dated you instead of him?"

"Yeah, something like that."

"Are you sure this is about me and not about Lisa? I know she was going with Phil before. In fact, I heard he and Charlie had a fight over her before Christmas. But that's not your problem."

"No. But—he still wants to date you."

"Well, I don't want to date him."

"He—he finds that a little hard to believe." So did I, but I wasn't going to say that to her.

"Glen." She was looking straight into my eyes. "Are you afraid of Charlie?"

"Uh—no, why would I be afraid of him?"

"I don't know. You seem to—" She smiled. "It's so crazy. Even if he beat you up fifty times, how would that make me go out with him?"

"Maybe you should tell that to Charlie," said that annoying voice from the front seat.

Nicole looked at Phil's back. "I suppose you are encouraging Glen to break up his friendship with Charlie."

"What's that supposed to mean?" Phil turned around to look at us.

"Watch the road!" I yelled. "She didn't mean anything. Did you, Nicole?"

"Well, I know that Phil has been antagonizing Charlie ever since he moved here."

"And Charlie hasn't done a thing, I suppose?" Phil sounded angry.

"I don't say Charlie is blameless. But it must be difficult when you're in your last year of school to move to a new town where you don't know anyone. I don't really think giving him a black eye is the best way to make him feel welcome."

"Wait a minute," I said. "Charlie is the one doing the threatening here."

"I don't for one moment believe he's serious. You're his best friend. Why would he want to fight you?"

I didn't know what else to say, so I did what my dad usually does when my mother makes a definite statement he doesn't want to touch. I remained silent.

"He's just annoyed because I wouldn't go out with him," Nicole said. "But he'll get over it."

I nodded. Yeah, he would get over it all right. After he finished with me.

Fortunately for all concerned, we pulled up at Nicole's house and she and Phil said good night. They were both polite, but kind of icy.

I walked her to the door.

On the way, she said, "I'm sorry Charlie has been annoying you because of me. I don't see how he could seriously believe I would go out with him even if he did persuade you to stop going with me. But I'm glad to know you aren't afraid of him."

I coughed. "Well, uh—"

"I'm proud of you," she said, "but I certainly won't be if you fight Charlie. I couldn't stand the thought of having two guys fighting over me. Anyway, now that you're a Christian, you couldn't fight him. The Bible says we're to turn the other cheek."

As if to emphasize her words, she kissed me on the cheek and went inside the house before I could say a word.

I felt kind of numb as I walked back to the car. Nicole was proud of me because I wasn't a coward. And she didn't want me to fight Charlie. In fact, she wouldn't like it if I did. Why didn't that seem helpful?

When I got into the front seat, Phil spat out, "What was that all about?" He mimicked Nicole's voice, "'I don't think giving him a black eye is the way to make him feel welcome.' What a—"

"She doesn't see the bad side of people."

"She always did think she was a little better than everybody else."

"Phil, I don't—"

"All right, I won't say anything more. Except this. I'm not getting involved with any more females. You never know how they're going to react and I can't be bothered trying to figure them out."

"I take it you and Lisa aren't getting back together."

"Like I'm going to go out with somebody who dumps me for Charlie the first chance she gets! And they're all the same. I tell you, I've had it! You'll find out. Nicole is no different from the rest of them!" He gunned the motor and we tore off down the street.

We drove the few blocks to my house in silence. Only not a pleasant silence, if you know what I mean. I was just plain confused. I had never seen Nicole act like that before. So—cold, I guess. As if she didn't like Phil.

They had often been in classes together, but I don't think they talked much. Phil had asked her out in the past, the same as most of the other guys, and she'd never gone with him. But she hadn't gone with most of the other guys either.

I couldn't think of any reason Nicole could have for disliking him. Until Charlie showed up, Phil was the most popular guy in our school.

It must have something to do with Charlie. Maybe Nicole did like him after all, and she was mad at Phil because he so obviously didn't.

"Uh-oh." Phil's voice intruded on my thoughts.

"What's wrong?"

Phil didn't answer, but he didn't need to. We had reached my house and Charlie's car was parked in his driveway and Charlie was leaning against it, arms crossed, like he was waiting for something. Or somebody.

Phil pulled into my driveway.

I would have ignored Charlie and gone inside the house, but with Phil already in a bad mood, that wasn't an option. Before I even got my door open, Phil had jumped out of the car and started across the street.

Charlie was moving too.

I know there's some expression about meeting people half-way, but I don't think this is what it means.

"Waiting for somebody?" Phil challenged. I thought of two gunfighters on Main Street at high noon.

"Nobody in particular," Charlie replied. Meaning me, of course. Mr. Nobody.

"Isn't it past your bed-time?" Phil sneered.

"As I matter of fact, I just got home from a date." Charlie's teeth gleamed in the streetlight and I knew he was smiling that smile of his that isn't really a smile. Not a nice smile, anyway. "I was with Lisa."

There were six feet between them when he said this. Phil covered those six feet in under a second and directed a clenched fist toward Charlie's nose.

Charlie brought his arm up, parried the blow, and plunged his left fist into Phil's stomach. Phil doubled over.

I had followed behind Phil without thinking. Now I stopped as Charlie moved toward me.

A voice in my mind said, "Run, sucker." But another voice said, "Hold it! What would Nicole think if you run?"

Charlie was right in front of me.

"Hit me if you want to," I said as bravely as I could. "I'll still go out with Nicole!"

I don't know what Charlie intended to do, because Phil leaped on him from behind.

The two went to the pavement, both punching wildly.

"Stop it!" I yelled. "Do you want to wake up the neighborhood?"

They were rolling around, Phil trying to get a headlock on Charlie and Charlie trying to get a scissors hold on Phil.

Neither one was succeeding.

Car lights appeared and I yelled, "There's a car coming! Get off the road."

I guess they thought I was making it up about the car, because they ignored me.

The car came closer. It was Mrs. Thornton's silver Chrysler. She pulled into her drive and I ran over and opened the car door. "It's Charlie and Phil. Can you stop them before they hurt each other?"

Mrs. Thornton is a very attractive blonde who looks as if she'd have trouble lifting a tea cup without strain, if you know what I mean. She didn't say a word to me. Just shut off the car, opened her purse and put the car keys inside, stepped out, pulled her white fur coat around her, and shut the car door.

Then she walked slowly over to the road, where Phil and Charlie were still going at it but good. Actually, Charlie had Phil kind of pinned, but as we came up Phil kneed him and managed to push him off. Phil was about to throw a hard right when Mrs. Thornton said, "Stop it right now." She didn't raise her voice. In fact, it was very low and quiet. But it seemed to pack a wallop. Phil's punch died in midair and Charlie rolled onto his knees and froze there, staring at his mother.

"I suppose you two think this is acceptable?" she continued in that misleadingly soft tone. "Rolling around in the dirt like a couple of animals? Look at your clothes. And your faces."

She turned toward Phil and eyed him in disgust. "I don't know about you, young man; perhaps this is normal for you. But my son is not used to this type of behavior. If I'd ever thought that coming to this—this morgue would mean my son had to lower himself to the level of the yokels who live here, I never would have agreed to the move. Young man, I don't want you anywhere near my son in the future. Do you understand?"

Without waiting for a reply, she turned on me. "Glen, I don't think your parents would be happy about your involvement in this, do you?"

I shook my head. Then I said, "No, Ma'am," because it seemed appropriate.

"Then stay away from Charles in the future. I'm sure he can find other friends, even in a place like this. Come, Charles."

At that, she adjusted her coat, turned on her flimsy high heels, and headed for her house.

Charlie got up. He didn't look at either of us as he followed her. Before they got into the house, we could hear her telling him to leave his filthy clothes in the laundry room and get into the shower before she would talk to him.

Phil and I looked at each other and started to laugh.

"No wonder Charlie is such an idiot," Phil said at last.

"Yeah. Look what he has to put up with at home," I agreed. Then I remembered something. "On the other hand, she isn't home a whole lot." Her interior decorating business is in Stanton, which is a city half an hour away. A lot of the time she works at night. Charlie's dad is a doctor, so he has long hours, too. The truth is, Charlie is alone at home a lot. In fact, once or twice I've even felt kind of sorry for him about that. Now I was thinking maybe he was better off if he was alone if that's what his mom is like.

I suddenly remembered the fight. "Are you okay?"

"Sure. I was winning. Would've had him if she hadn't come along just then."

Yeah, right. More likely they would have gone on for another hour without a clear winner.

"I've got to do something about this," I said aloud.

"What do you mean?" Phil was hitting his clothes to remove the dust from the road.

"Well, I can't go around ducking from Charlie for the rest of my life. I'll have to have it out with him. I'm not going to give up Nicole because he's threatened me. And she's not going to date him anyway. It's all so stupid!"

"Yeah, and if he does date Nicole, what's he going to do about Lisa?" Phil said bitterly. "Not that I care. I hope he dumps her the same way she dumped me."

Lisa is a fairly tall, very attractive girl with short dark brown hair and a great figure. Mom said once she is "perky"—whatever that means. She talks a lot, is involved in everything, and is the head cheerleader. She goes through guys like she was buying lottery tickets.

"Lisa dumps everybody eventually, Phil," I said in my newfound wisdom with girls.

"Yeah, I know. I should go for somebody dependable. Like Joyce, right?" He grinned, and I knew he was baiting me.

Okay, maybe Joyce isn't his type. But she is a Christian, which is good. The only problem is Phil isn't a Christian.

A new thought suddenly hit me. What could I do to show Phil he needs God in his life more than he needs a new girlfriend?

# 4

The next morning was Saturday. Nicole and I had agreed to meet at the library at ten to work on an essay we had to write for history, so I did the jobs Mom wanted done in a hurry. I don't mean that quite the way it sounds. She didn't *want* them done in a hurry. I *did* them in a hurry, because I wanted to leave. Oh, you know what I mean.

I hadn't bothered to say anything about going to the library to Phil. I figured he would be too stiff and sore to manage anyway.

I walked, and Nicole was waiting when I arrived.

"Hi, Glen," she said. "Dad had to get groceries so he dropped me off. We could have picked you up, but I didn't think of it."

"No problem," I said. "So, do you want to go for a Coke first?"

"No way," she laughed. "I know you. Anything to get out of work."

I smiled back rather sheepishly.

We found a table in a corner where we wouldn't bother anyone else.

Charlie came in about ten minutes later. I wondered if he'd followed me.

He looked okay, considering. Phil must not have landed any major punches. Not on his face anyway. There was a reddish patch on his cheek, but that could have been from scraping it on the road.

He was apparently looking for a book on a shelf near us. I ignored him and so did Nicole. Of course, he might have come to work and not to spy on us, but still—his presence made me very nervous.

After a while he wandered away, and a short time later Nicole left for a moment to go to the washroom.

Like magic, Charlie appeared. He came to a stop across from me, behind the chair Nicole had been using. "So," he said, "having a good time, Glen?"

"We're working," I said.

"Sure you are. What else would *you* be doing?" He put a lot of emphasis on the 'you.'

I stared at the book in front of me.

"About last night—"

I looked up, expecting some kind of comment about his mother.

"It isn't going to work, Glen."

"Huh?"

"Phil can't be around to protect you all the time."

This wasn't what I was expecting. And I was tired of his threats. "Big deal," I said. I pretended I was reading the book Nicole had found for me.

"Look, you can't keep this up," he said.

"What are you talking about now?"

"You and Nicole. You know you can't handle her."

"I wouldn't try to 'handle' her."

"You don't know anything about girls!"

"I never pretended I did," I said quietly, aware that there were other people in the room who might be able to hear. "Why don't you give it a rest, Charlie?"

He came around the table to where I was sitting. "Why don't you stand up and say that?"

I looked at him. "I'm busy."

"Chicken, chicken, chicken," he taunted. "That's why Nicole likes you, I guess. She wants a wimp who does what he's told. Not a man."

When I didn't say anything, he grabbed the book I was reading and threw it to the floor. "Got the guts to come and pick it up?" he asked. He was smiling.

I shook my head. "I'm not that stupid."

"Not man enough, either."

"Charlie—"

"Wimp."

"I'm not fighting you, Charlie. There's no point. I don't understand why you think beating me up would impress Nicole."

"I don't think anything of the sort. I just want to beat you up because you're a two-timing rat who went behind my back and stole my girl!"

"She never was your girl!"

"She would have been if you hadn't gone behind my back!" Face red, eyes blazing, hands clenched into fists, he leaned toward me and without thinking I stood up and took an involuntary step backwards. Charlie pushed my chair into the table. I took another step backward. Inside I began to pray, "God, help! What should I do?"

As Charlie swung, I took a dive—sprawling on the tiled floor in a heap.

Before anything else could happen, Nicole hurried over yelling, "Glen! Are you okay? Charlie, what did you to do him? You leave him alone!"

Charlie backed off.

"Are you hurt, Glen?" She knelt beside me.

I shook my head and started to get up. Nicole put her arm around me to help. Charlie stood watching us with his hands on his hips.

As I regained my feet, she turned on Charlie, "What did you do to him?"

"I didn't do anything!" Charlie sounded exasperated. "The stupid jerk just—" More calmly, he added, "Why would I want to hurt my best friend?"

Nicole's eyes met his. "You didn't knock him down?"

"Of course not. He fell over his own feet."

She stared at me. "Glen?"

I mumbled the words, "I tripped." Okay, it wasn't exactly true. I had decided that the only way I could avoid being hit by Charlie was if I were already on the floor.

Nicole looked from me to Charlie and back to me before saying, "We'd better all get to work."

Charlie shrugged. "Suit yourself. See you later, Glen."

I realized people were staring at us, so I picked up the book Charlie had thrown on the floor and sat down. Nicole sat across from me and leaned forward. "What really happened?" she whispered.

"Not much," I said. "He's just a little annoyed because you're with me instead of him."

"Did you really trip?"

"I was just getting out of his way."

"Are you okay?"

"Sure. I'm not made of glass."

"You're sure you weren't fighting?"

"Positive."

We went back to work, and no more was said. But I knew that sooner or later I was going to have to face up to Charlie. If I did fight him, what would Nicole say?

Around one, we went over to Harry's to get some burgers. The Peabody Diner is always closed after Christmas until April because the couple who own it go to Arizona for the worst part of the winter. So there aren't many choices of where to go. My friends and I have always gone to Harry's.

Nicole had to be home early because her family was going to visit a relative in a town about an hour's drive away. Some great uncle was having an eightieth birthday or something. So after lunch we walked to her place.

We took a roundabout way—to the outskirts of town and down a path I knew beside a little pond. The pond was iced over, but not solid enough to walk on. Some of the trees had snow in their upper branches, so there was a lot of white mixed in with the browns of the bare tree trunks, bits of green from a sprinkling of evergreens, and patches of clear blue sky overhead. The only sound was the crunching of snow underfoot as Nicole and I walked along.

Everything was calm and peaceful and untroubled here. But of course it wouldn't last long. In a few months this quiet spot would be alive with red-winged blackbirds building nests, chickadees singing, frogs croaking, and crickets chirping. Last year, I'd spotted a beaver and his family here, all working hard. Everything would be green and alive, with a rainbow of flowers.

"You'll have to think of something," Nicole said.

"What?" I asked cautiously, realizing she had been talking to me.

"To help him understand," she replied.

"Understand?" I echoed, totally puzzled.

"You know. How God works." There was a pause as she looked at me. "Weren't you listening?"

I was feeling guilty about not quite telling the truth back at the library, so this time I went with honesty. "No. I was thinking about this place and how it changes with the seasons. All white and quiet, now; green and alive in the spring."

"Why, Glen, that's great!"

"Uh, yeah, I guess it is."

"Of course it is. I had no idea you were poetic!"

"Huh?"

"You are."

"If you say so. But nobody else would agree. Besides, poets are wimps."

"No way. David was a poet."

"David who?" I groped in my mind. The only David I could think of was the kid who delivered our paper. "You mean David Crane?"

She laughed. "No, silly, I mean King David. From the Bible." Seeing the blank look on my face, she added, "The boy who killed the giant, Goliath."

"I never heard of him. No, wait a minute. Did he use a slingshot?"

"Yes."

"Yeah, I guess I must have heard it somewhere."

"Well, he became king of the Jewish nation, and he was a mighty warrior. But he also wrote most of the book of psalms in the Bible—and it's all songs and poems."

"Yeah?"

"So it can't be bad to be poetic, because God called David a 'man after his own heart.'"

"I guess," I said doubtfully. But I thought it was wise to change the subject. "What were you saying about Charlie?"

"Just that he needs help. He doesn't know God, does he?"

I shook my head. But then I felt I needed to add something. "He knows what he's heard in church, but he was only going there to impress you. I don't think he really has any idea about God or Jesus."

"That's what I thought. So you'll have to find a way to tell him."

My feet stopped in mid-stride and I turned to stare at her. "Me?" I blurted out. "Me tell Charlie about God?"

"Well, who else? You're his friend, so he'll listen to you."

"I don't think so."

"You mean you won't do it?" She sounded surprised.

"I mean he wouldn't listen to me."

"But you have to try. That's all God asks us to do. Try."

"I guess. But he's pretty happy just the way he is."

"But at least you'll have tried."

She was so earnest that I couldn't very well say no. So I promised her I'd try to talk to Charlie about Jesus the first chance I got, and then I was so desperate to change the subject that I suggested we hurry so she wouldn't be late.

I got back to my house at a quarter after three. Ten minutes later the phone rang. It was Phil.

"What? You're actually there? I figured you'd be with Nicole."

"I was, but she's gone for the rest of the day."

"I wondered about taking in a movie tonight in Stanton."

"What's showing?"

He gave me the title of the latest cop action thriller.

"Sounds good," I said.

"Pick you up at seven?"

"Sure."

"You're allowed to go?"

Puzzled, I said, "Yeah."

"Shouldn't you check first?"

I was still puzzled. "Mom and Dad don't care if I go to a movie."

"I wasn't thinking about your mom and dad."

"I don't get it."

"I wasn't sure Nicole would let you go."

"What's that supposed to mean?"

"I thought maybe you had to ask her permission."

"Very funny," I replied. "Should I hang up now, or do you really want to go to a movie?"

"Oh, I'm going, and you can come if you want, but won't she be mad?"

It had never occurred to me that Nicole might expect me to stop going to movies or dances because she hardly ever goes. Maybe she would. But it wasn't something I wanted to discuss with Phil.

"See you at seven." I hung up.

But I had a lot on my mind. Asking Jesus to come into my life and take over had made a lot of sense when I did it just before Christmas. But what were the implications? Did it mean I couldn't have fun any more? And what would happen if I did something God didn't like? Would he go back out of my life?

Since I didn't have answers to any of my questions, and my head was starting to hurt from all that heavy stuff, I watched wrestling on TV until dinner.

Phil's beat-up car arrived in front of my house at roughly 7:10. I took my time going out and getting in the back with Brett. Mac was in front with Phil.

Mac and Brett are kind of inseparable. They live next door to each other and do everything together. But they look kind of strange together. Mac is short and skinny and Brett is about 5' 10"—my height—and about 30 pounds overweight.

For most of the half hour ride we talked about school and stuff. Just as we were nearing the city, Brett said innocently, "So she didn't give you a hard time about coming, huh?"

"You guys are sick."

"You have to admit you've barely been apart from her since Christmas," Mac teased from the front.

"When I think about last summer and how you used to complain about Phil's spending all his time with Lisa...." Brett groaned.

"You guys must have awfully dull lives. Mostly what Nicole has been doing is helping me with my homework and essays and stuff."

"Oh, yeah, sure." Phil's voice oozed sarcasm.

"Wait till you see the marks I'm going to get this year. You guys will all faint."

"You found a way to cheat without getting caught?" Mac asked.

"No." I was getting annoyed.

Brett looked at me, his head cocked to one side. "Well, there's something different about you. You never used to get mad."

"I'm not mad," I said.

"You've really been studying?" Mac asked. His voice was no longer teasing.

"Really," I said.

"Wow!" Mac whistled.

"Aw, let's go see the movie," Phil said as he parked the car.

We went in, found seats near the back, and sat down to relax. But every so often I felt one of them staring at me like I might suddenly explode or something. It was weird.

So was the movie. I mean it was the usual cops and bad guys and a bit of sex thrown in between the car chases and all, but I found it kind of unreal. The truth was I'd probably have found studying with Nicole more interesting. And that isn't me.

Had I changed? If I had, I knew it wasn't really because of Nicole. She'd helped, but the real change was asking God to take control of my life.

My thoughts suddenly made me forget the movie, and I realized with a burst of excitement that it wasn't a question of not being allowed to do certain things, but of God's taking away the desire. Watching the movie wasn't wrong; it was just a waste of time. And it was teaching a lot of wrong values—you know, the "shoot first, ask questions later" kind of mentality. Maybe I just didn't need it.

Later, we went for drinks and fries and then Phil drove home, dropping Mac and Brett off first. I was in the front seat now, like I'd always been before last summer and Phil's preoccupation with Lisa. It felt good.

He stopped in front of my house, but I didn't get out right away. There were no lights on at Charlie's. I wondered where he was.

"Glen?" Phil asked.

"Yeah?"

"You look like you're someplace else."

"Huh?"

"We're at your house."

"Oh, yeah. Sorry." I started to open the door, then hesitated. "I was just thinking about Charlie."

"What about him?"

"Oh, I don't know."

I was reluctant to tell him what I was thinking. He would likely laugh. But I decided to chance it. "You know what, Phil? I kind of feel sorry for him."

Phil snorted. "Don't waste your time. What doesn't he have that he wants—except Nicole?"

"You're just sore because of Lisa."

"Wait till he steals your girl."

"He couldn't 'steal' her unless she wanted to go."

"Thanks."

"Lisa isn't good enough for you, Phil."

"Oh, yeah? So who does the expert, Glen Sauten, think is good enough?"

"What about Joyce?"

"Oh, gee, thanks. You really have a high opinion of me, don't you?"

"Why? She may not be the best-looking girl in school, but she isn't bad. And she's smart. Didn't you have fun last night?"

"Glen, are you feeling okay?"

"What's the matter?"

"To be polite, let's just say she isn't my type and leave it there."

"What's wrong with her?"

"Spoken like the guy who's going with the best-looking girl in the school."

"I don't like Nicole because of how she looks."

"That's easy to say."

"It's true."

"Well, the way she looks makes it a lot easier to like her."

"Okay, what about Marta?"

"What about her?"

"Would you say she's good-looking?"

"Yeah."

"You ever wanted to date her?"

"Not a chance."

"Me, neither. Because she may look good, but underneath she's poison."

"So what?"

"So, if you don't want to date Marta because she's a creep, why not date Joyce because she's nice even though she isn't as good-looking? You're saying a girl has to be good-looking *and* nice to get your interest. Not that I'd say Lisa was so nice."

"She's good-looking."

"Next to Nicole, she's the best-looking girl in town. But what if, next to Nicole, Joyce was the nicest girl?"

Phil was glaring at me. I inched closer to the door, ready to exit fast if necessary.

"So Joyce is nice," Phil said finally. "Why should I care? And, from what I know about her and Nicole, why should I want to date somebody who doesn't ever have fun?"

"Not true."

"I think you've been brainwashed. First by Charlie, now by Nicole. Maybe doctors should do tests on you—'pushover of the month' or something. You believe anything Charlie or Nicole tells you."

"I'm not that dumb."

"Are you planning on sleeping in my car?"

I opened the door. "Thanks for inviting me to go along."

"If I'd known I was going to get a lecture along with the movie, I wouldn't have bothered."

Don't ask me where I got the nerve, but the next thing I said was, "So, are you picking me up in the morning?"

"Tomorrow's Sunday. Why should I pick you up?"

"To take me to church."

"Don't push your luck, Sauten. Going out with you and Nicole and Joyce is bad enough. But if you think I'm going to church with you—well, let's just say I'd rather deliver you to Charlie and watch him beat you up. So if you want to go to church in the morning, you go right ahead. Me, I sleep in Sunday mornings."

He impatiently raced the motor, so without another word, I shut my door and watched him squeal his tires as he backed out of the driveway and tore off down the street.

I was up and ready for church early. Mom and Dad were in the kitchen eating breakfast and reading the Stanton Free Press. They didn't say much. I knew Mom had been kind of dejected the last couple of days because she hadn't found a job yet.

In a town the size of Wallace, it doesn't take long to check out all the possibilities.

Yesterday Mom had said something at dinner about maybe volunteering at the hospital or something. I have to confess I felt pretty good about it. I really wasn't anxious for her to get a job. I know it's selfish, but I kind of like knowing she'll be there when I come home from school. I like the cookies she bakes and other things she does because she has time. I sure didn't want her to turn into something like Charlie's mom. Or even Phil's. Mrs. Trent works as a clerk in the bigger grocery store in town. (Bigger is the right word here, because there are only two grocery stores in town. See, I am learning something. Nicole was just telling me yesterday about using "er" when you're comparing two things and "est" when you're comparing three.) Anyway, the point I wanted to make is that the Trents eat a lot of frozen dinners and things like that. Cookies out of bags instead of cookie jars. Pies that come out of cardboard boxes and taste like it. I guess I'm spoiled all right, but I like it that way.

Dad said I could take the car to church, so I did. I sat next to Nicole during the worship service and afterwards in the youth group. It felt pretty good. Derek and Andy and the other guys who Nicole has gone out with a time or two looked annoyed, and I can't say that didn't make me feel even better.

Charlie wasn't there. He'd started coming to church to impress Nicole, and I'd come because he dragged me, but I guess he wasn't playing games any more. What he hadn't bargained on was my realizing that there really is a God, and that Jesus Christ died for me—well, for *everyone*, but we each have to accept him into our life.

Thinking about that got me thinking about Charlie again and how he didn't seem to understand that bit. Or Phil. He didn't know the first thing about God. His mom went to mass occasionally, but I don't think Phil or his dad were ever inside a church.

The singing and stuff was okay, and the sermon was good. It was about Jonah who got swallowed by a big fish because he didn't want to obey God. That made me feel guilty again. If only I knew why God was letting me get into this mess with Phil and Charlie—! While the people were singing at the end, I was silently praying, asking God to show me what he wanted me to do.

I guess I didn't hear a lot about what was said in the youth group afterwards. To tell the truth, I sometimes found it pretty boring—even since I'd become a Christian. We had lesson books and all, and we were studying the Bible, but—I guess it was me, but it just didn't seem particularly interesting. Oh, sometimes what Mr. Reiss was teaching was good, but I just couldn't get past the thought that I didn't know anybody here. I mean, I knew them because we were all in high school and we live in a small town and all. I'd been coming to the class now for roughly four months. But—I didn't really *know* anybody. I mean, like how come some of the kids acted differently at school? Did they ever have any problems? They didn't seem to. They all seemed happy enough—although, to tell the truth, sometimes some of them seemed bored, too. But likely I just didn't know enough yet.

I went to the Grants' for lunch. There was a new couple there, too—John and Katherine Hamilton. They had moved to Wallace after Christmas. John was a little taller than me, solid, with brown skin, black curly hair, and a weather-beaten look. He was a mechanic who had come to work in Carl Winter's Garage. Carl had been operating it alone since his son moved to Stanton to work in a bigger garage there. Carl was getting older and needed some help, so it was good this new guy had come to work for him. John's wife Katherine had been a kindergarten teacher but wasn't working now. She was fairly tall—nearly as tall as me. Her skin was darker than John's, but she had short reddish hair arranged in clusters of curls, and gold-rimmed glasses. She was wearing a loose dress and even I could tell she was expecting a baby soon.

Both of the Hamiltons seemed kind of—different. I don't mean because they were Afro-American, though in our small town that certainly did make them different. But what I really thought was different was how they talked about God—like he was right there all the time. Once, John said something that even Pastor Grant seemed to find surprising. Mrs. Grant had cooked a couple of chickens and mashed potatoes and vegetables, and we were just finishing when John—Mr. Hamilton said I could call him that—and Pastor Grant got talking about getting people to meet in small groups.

They both seemed to think that the groups were a good idea, but Pastor Grant's idea of them seemed to be mainly about having some of the church people get together on a week-night to learn more about the Bible, which sounded to me a lot like the Sunday youth class.

John seemed to be talking about another kind of small group, where people got together to share personal stuff and help each other in their day-to-day lives. I had been talking to Nicole and one of her little sisters, but I started listening when I heard him say, "People won't grow unless they talk about real-life issues with other believers." That was sort of what I'd been thinking. Having people talk about real-life things that matter to them, I mean.

Anyway, the next thing you know, John looked past the table at the wall behind Mrs. Grant and said, "What do you think, Lord? Should we talk about this now?"

Everybody stared at him.

# 5

Then came the really strange part. He nodded, and said, "Yes, you're right. I'll wait." Like God had answered his question! I turned to look, but all I saw was a beige wall with a picture of an old country house hanging on it.

Pastor Grant coughed and asked Mrs. Grant if he should get the dessert. She jumped up and asked Nicole to help her clear the table.

Nicole's brother, Paul, who is a couple of years younger than her, got up too, to get dessert dishes.

That left me at the table with the Hamiltons and the two younger girls, who were arguing about something else, oblivious to what had just happened.

"So, Glen, you're in your last year of school?" John asked.

I looked at him, and I saw hands stained with grease that was so deep no soap would ever get it all out, and dark brown eyes with a mischievous twinkle in them. My mind went back to my grandfather—my dad's dad—who'd had similar hands, except the stains on his wrinkled and callused hands weren't from being a mechanic, but from fifty years of farming. But the twinkle was the same. I found myself smiling.

"Yeah," I said, remembering his question. "My last year."

"Any plans?"

"Not really. My parents seem to think I'm going to college, though."

"You aren't sure?"

I shook my head.

"Well, God will direct you in his own time," John said. "You do know him, don't you?"

I felt my face turning red. "Yeah, sort of—I mean, not very long. Just since before Christmas, really."

"That's wonderful!" Katherine said.

John echoed the word, adding, "Do you have someone discipling you?"

I had no idea what he was talking about, so it was good that Pastor Grant walked in just then, carrying a chocolate cake. "I've been doing a little of that myself," he said, "but nothing too official."

That got them off on another discussion which left me totally lost, so I concentrated on my cake and then argued about hockey with Paul. But afterwards, as I drove home, I remembered that twinkle and the feeling it had given me, and I prayed silently that God would direct me in his good time, just as John said.

It's funny. I've never really known anyone who was black. I mean known as to talk with much. In our whole town we have only a handful of people of black or oriental or East Indian ancestry. There are maybe a dozen all together, and I don't know most of them very well. I go to school with a few, of course, and I have no problem with them. I just have never had much opportunity to really get to know them. I was kind of curious about John and Katherine. A little because they were black, but more because they seemed to know God better than anyone I'd met—maybe even better than Pastor Grant.

As I stepped into our house, I was feeling more relaxed than I had for ages. Mom and Dad had apparently gone for a walk, or maybe to visit Mrs. Pearson, as they often did on Sunday. I changed into jeans and a T-shirt and was just about to see what was on TV when the phone rang. It was Brett.

"Glen, you've got to get over to Harry's. Hurry!"

"What's going on?" I yelled, but he had already hung up.

I stood in the kitchen wondering if this was some kind of joke. I couldn't imagine Brett's doing anything to set me up. Had Phil told him to call? But that didn't make sense.

The car was sitting in the drive and I had the keys.

As I drove down Main Street, I could see a crowd outside the cafe. When I got close enough, I realized Phil and Charlie were in the center of the crowd. They seemed to be arguing.

I parked and ran across the street.

"Glen, maybe you can talk some sense into them!" Brett yelled as he ran over to me.

"What's going on?"

"They're nuts!" somebody else yelled.

I pushed through the crowd. Phil's face was red and angry-looking. "You're nothing but a city jerk! You came here because you thought all of us small-town people would bow at your feet. Well, we won't!"

"Come on, Phil," I said, grabbing his arm. "Leave him alone."

He pushed me away.

"Stay out of this!" Charlie said. "We don't need any wimps involved."

I ignored him. "Phil! Come on. He likes getting you mad."

Phil spoke through clenched teeth. "You heard him, Glen. Stay out of it. You don't belong here."

"You're just protecting me!" I yelled, forgetting that people might hear.

"Like fun I am! I'm trying to cut this city jerk down to the right size!"

"Yeah, well you—you—" Charlie's face was so red I thought he might explode. He couldn't even think of words bad enough to get his feelings across. He swore. Finally, he settled for, "You don't even know how to dress yourself to look like a human being! You're nothing but one of those—those straw-chewing bumpkins out of the movies!"

"You—!" Phil summed up his thoughts in syllables that were unprintable.

"Yeah? Why don't you put your money where your mouth is?"

"What are you talking about?"

"Your car."

"What about it?"

"You're so proud of that bunch of metal and rusted bolts. Why don't you race me?"

"My car could beat yours any day of the week!"

"Stop it, you idiots! Somebody will get hurt!"

I could have saved my breath; neither of them paid any attention to me.

"When?" Charlie asked.

"Now," Phil replied in a Clint Eastwood kind of voice. I half-expected him to add, "Make my day."

"Where?"

Somebody yelled, "The old air strip!" and all of a sudden the whole crowd took off, those who didn't have cars racing to get seats with friends who did. Phil yelled, "Follow me!" to Charlie and went for his car. Forgetting all about having our car, I hurried after Phil. As he started the motor, I jerked open the passenger door. He burned rubber getting out of there, and I more or less fell into the front seat.

I was still trying to get the door shut and find my seat belt as we left the town limits and picked up speed. When I finally felt satisfied that I was actually in the car, I looked back. Five or six cars, including Charlie's, were following. We looked like a parade. Or a funeral. Except we were driving too fast for either.

The old air strip is about five minutes out of town. It was used a long time ago as a training camp for the air force, but over the years the runways have become broken and overgrown with weeds. Despite that, it's been popular as a place for drag racing. Just a couple of years ago Barney Sorenson was killed there while racing his motorcycle. Phil knew that, and I couldn't believe he'd be so dumb.

I told him as much, but all he did was turn up the radio.

"Don't be an idiot!" I yelled.

He ignored me.

I turned down the radio. "You're my bodyguard. What kind of bodyguard will you be if you get yourself killed?"

He turned the radio back up, yelling as he did, "I know how to drive."

"You can still get hurt!" I was screaming now.

We reached the air strip and he stopped the car. "You'd better get out."

"No! It could be icy, Phil. Stop being so stupid!"

Charlie came to Phil's window. Phil turned down the radio.

"Start is at the other end. Finish is right here." Phil pointed to a faint line in the pavement that someone had painted so people could practice parallel parking. My dad had taught me to drive here, as had most other people's dads.

"Don't be idiots, you guys!" I yelled the words, but no one seemed to hear me.

Phil was still talking to Charlie, in a loud voice so the crowd that had gathered would hear. "I win, you leave Glen alone and forget about Nicole. I'd say you stop being such a jerk, but that would be impossible."

"After I win, as I will, you agree to stop protecting Glen, and you stay out of my way in the future." Charlie's voice was cool and confident. "Like my mother said, you're a bad influence."

"You creep!" Phil said a few other words, which I won't repeat, and then he looked over at me. "Get out!"

"Phil, you can't do this. You have no right—"

He emphasized the words like he was talking to a person who was totally deaf. "Get out!"

Phil raced the motor. I sat there, torn. Finally, reluctantly, I undid the seat belt and opened the door. I tried one more shot. "What do you think your parents would say if they knew you were going to race him?"

He glared at me and gunned it. I had to jump from the car, slamming the door as I fell. He led Charlie's car to the starting line, which was about a half-mile away.

I sat on the cold snow-covered cement.

"Can't you stop them?" Brett said as he and Mac ran up. Like Nicole, he seemed to have weird ideas of my capabilities.

Anyway, there was no more time. At a signal I didn't hear, the two cars began moving, gathering speed, until they were the center of a great cloud of snow and exhaust. They were neck and neck, and you could barely tell them apart, Charlie's shiny red Mustang and Phil's old green Goose, shooting toward the finish line, getting closer and larger all the time. But suddenly the cloud split in two, one part flying toward us; the other veering to the right in a spinning frenzy as the Goose hit the edge of the runway and rolled over and over onto the neighboring field.

No one was watching as Charlie's car hit the finish line. We were all staring at Phil's car as it settled with a final bounce right-side-up on the field.

Tires squealing, Charlie made a tight U-turn and raced back down the runway with the rest of us running after.

Before we were even close, Charlie had slammed to a stop and was out of his car, scrambling over the snowy field.

We could all see him struggling to open Phil's door, then suddenly yanking it right off its hinges. He reached inside and got hold of Phil, dragging him out and carrying him away from the car just seconds before there was a ball of fire from near the gas tank and Phil's old Goose exploded into a searing bonfire.

As if the crowd was one person, we pulled up, none of us believing what had just happened in front of our eyes. It was the sort of thing you see all the time on the screen, but you never believe can happen in real life.

And then, as if it were choreographed, we remembered Phil, and the whole bunch of us ran to where he was lying on the ground with Charlie bent over him.

There was blood all over his jacket and his face. The part of his face that wasn't red with blood was white. I thought he was dead and my stomach did a sudden lurch that left me hanging onto the nearest person so my legs wouldn't give way. I saw Charlie pull off his jacket and throw it over Phil's legs and rip off his own T-shirt so he could roll it into a pad which he pressed against Phil's chest.

Somebody yelled, "Derek's calling for help on his cell phone," and then I was kneeling at Phil's other side and taking off my own shirt to wipe the blood off his face.

The others stood around, but no one spoke. The only sounds were Charlie's breathing, which, because of his exertion, was coming in gasps, and the hoarse, labored sound of Phil's irregular breaths.

"Hold this down," Charlie ordered. I put my hand on the pad he'd made and held it firmly on the place where blood was seeping out of a gash in Phil's chest. Charlie took Phil's pulse and then lifted each of his eyelids.

"How is he?" I asked. My voice sounded weak and hoarse—I would never have recognized it as mine.

"I hope the ambulance gets here in a hurry," he said.

"Derek called for help," someone repeated. Charlie grunted.

Then he muttered, more to himself than anyone else. "I should never have moved him."

"You had to!" I exclaimed. "Look what happened!"

"I think his back's hurt. Moving him likely made it worse."

"You had no choice." I looked again at Phil's white face. "Isn't there anything else we can do?"

"You tell me."

I looked down at the compress I was holding. It seemed to me the blood was easing up. Was that good or bad?

"Charlie?"

"Yeah?"

"His breathing doesn't sound good."

"You noticed."

"What should we do?"

"You know how to give CPR?"

"No."

"Then don't worry about it."

"Should we try?"

"Not unless he stops breathing."

We kept watching his face and listening to his labored breathing until, at last, the sound of a distant siren broke the silence. Then another.

In no time a police car and an ambulance came hurtling toward us and screeched to a standstill next to Charlie's car. The two men from the ambulance raced to get a stretcher from the back and then scrambled across the field.

At the first sound of the sirens, most of the kids had headed for their cars. I guess they had remembered that drag racing wasn't exactly encouraged by the police.

By the time the police and the stretcher reached us, only Charlie, Brett, Mac, and I were left. We watched as the ambulance attendants took over. When Charlie mentioned a possible back injury, they got out a special brace to put on Phil before they moved him to the stretcher. They checked him over, started an intravenous, put on an oxygen mask, and carried him to the ambulance.

The police officers stood staring at what was left of Phil's car and shaking their heads.

I looked at Charlie. He was sitting on the ground, shirtless and shivering, his face and body and even his hair streaked with sweat and dirt and blood. I didn't know whether to punch him for being such a jerk or hug him for getting Phil out of the car before it exploded.

I don't think Sergeant Speck or Officer Crammer knew what to do either.

They questioned us briefly. Brett and Mac did most of the talking—going over the argument back at Harry's, and Charlie's challenging Phil to a race, and then Charlie's saving Phil's life. Finally, Sergeant Speck said we'd better get our coats on and all go to the hospital. I suddenly realized that I was also sitting there with no shirt or coat on, and I was half-frozen.

Brett and Mac rode in the squad car with Sergeant Speck. I rode in the back of Charlie's car with Charlie in the front and Officer Crammer driving. None of us said anything. I guess we were all wondering if Phil was going to live. I was also wondering whether this was my fault. And thinking over what I'd like to do to Charlie.

We all went into Emergency together. But as we got inside, Charlie brushed past the rest of us, and I heard him telling the nurse at the desk that he had to see his dad. She said he'd have to wait; that his dad was in surgery. So he sat on a chair in the waiting area at the far end of the row.

Brett, Mac, and I sat down, too. I don't know about them, but my knees felt like they couldn't hold me up at all.

Officer Crammer phoned Phil's parents and then drove over to get them.

Sergeant Speck stayed with us.

I knew I should phone home, but I wasn't sure my voice would work. All I could think of was Phil lying there, his face white and bloody. What if he died without my ever having a chance to tell him about God?

I looked at Charlie. He was leaning with his elbows on his knees, his head bent and his eyes staring at the white and black tiled floor.

"How could you have been so stupid?" The words startled me. Especially when I realized it was me talking.

He glared at me, "I suppose it's all my fault?"

"Most of it is."

"Phil always over-reacts."

"You had no business doing what you did!"

"He's supposed to be a good driver."

"He *is* a good driver!"

"So why couldn't he keep his car on the pavement?"

"You know as well as I do you were both going too fast for a place like that! There were patches of ice!"

"Aw, so what. He'll be okay."

"Sure he will. Then what will you do?"

"What's that supposed to mean?"

"All you've done since you moved here is cause problems!"

"Getting brave, aren't you? Especially with Phil not here to fight for you."

"I can fight my own fights!"

"Yeah? Since when?"

I jumped up and walked over. "Since right now!" I stood there awkwardly, wondering how you hit someone who's sitting down.

I'd forgotten about Officer Speck. "Cool it, Glen. We've had enough excitement for today, I think." He took my shoulder and led me back to my seat.

I was shaking when I sat down, whether because of the cold or the shock or because I couldn't believe what I'd just done, I don't know.

A nurse came to talk to Sergeant Speck. I recognized her as Darlene's mom. Darlene is a friend of Nicole's.

"Are you waiting because of Phil Trent?" she asked. "He's not in immediate danger, but he'll be in surgery for a while. There's not much point in your staying here."

Sergeant Speck came over to us. "You kids can go home. I'll come and talk to you if I need more information. "You," he was looking at Charlie, "is your mother at home?"

Charlie shook his head. "She had a meeting."

"Here in town?"

"In Stanton."

"Well, then, I think you'd better come down to the station with me."

Brett and Mac walked the six blocks from the hospital to Harry's with me to pick up my car. Then I drove them home. When I got to my house, I gave Mom and Dad a quick summary of what had happened. They were both shocked.

"Why were they racing?" Dad asked me for the third or fourth time.

"Mostly because they've never liked each other." I had sort of skimmed over the part about Charlie and Nicole and I that had been the real origin of the fight.

"I can't believe either of them would do something so foolish!" Mom said for the fifth or sixth time.

Dad and I agreed with her, and then I went to wash the blood off and get a new shirt.

We had dinner, but it had no taste. Then we sat for a while, not saying much. Mom decided she was going to the hospital to be with Phil's parents. I turned the television on but I didn't really watch it. I mostly sat there drinking a root beer and thinking about Phil. After a while, I started praying silently that he'd be okay, and that I would have a chance to talk to both him and Charlie about God. And that they would listen.

I must have been sitting there two hours or more without moving when the phone rang.

Dad was in the kitchen, so he answered it and talked for a few minutes. When he had hung up, he came to the doorway. "That was your mother, Glen. She phoned to let us know that Phil is not in danger."

"Is he okay, Dad?"

"He has concussion, and he needed stitches for cuts on his head and chest, and two of his ribs were broken, and there was a lot of bruising, and—" his voice broke.

"What is it, Dad?"

"There was some kind of injury to his lower back. It seems he has no feeling in his legs."

"No feeling?"

"There was damage to his spine and to the spinal cord. They've operated. But there's a good chance he won't be able to walk. There's also trauma."

"Trauma?"

"Basically, the shock of what happened. It can affect a lot of things."

"Is he conscious?"

"He was. But I think they gave him something to make him sleep."

"How about his mom and dad?"

"Your mom says they're pretty shaken, but they're going to go home and get some sleep now."

"Oh."

"You'd better get to bed, Glen."

"Yeah. Okay, Dad."

My last thought before I fell into a troubled sleep was to wonder how on earth Phil would ever believe God loved him if he had no feeling in his legs!

The next morning came and went. It was nearly eleven when I woke up. I really had been tired! I showered and dressed and tried to forget what had happened the night before. As if I could.

I found a note from Mom on the kitchen table. She'd let me sleep in on purpose. She'd talked to the hospital and they said Phil was in stable condition and that no visitors would be allowed today. She'd gone to get groceries so she could make some food for Phil's parents.

I made myself a sandwich and then walked to school for the afternoon classes. Just as I got to the sidewalk out front, I saw Nicole coming, so I waited for her.

"Hi," she said. "I missed you this morning."

"Nobody woke me up."

"I take it you know about Phil?"

"I was there."

"You were? Then why on earth didn't you stop them?"

"I tried."

"They say Charlie saved Phil's life."

"He did. After putting him in danger in the first place."

"Are you saying the accident was Charlie's fault?"

"Not exactly, but—" Did I tell Nicole that I thought Phil was only trying to get Charlie off my back? Just looking after the boy. "Phil knew Charlie was threatening me. We talked about that. I think he was trying to get Charlie to leave me alone."

"By racing his car against Charlie's?" Her voice was scornful. "I don't know much about cars, but I would have thought there was no possible way Phil's car could win a race against Charlie's. It was old and beat-up. He was stupid to even try."

I couldn't argue with that. I would have been totally surprised if Phil had won the race. But I couldn't very well tell her that when Phil got mad he often did things without stopping to think. That would sure make her think better of him.

"I certainly don't want Phil to be hurt, and I hope he's okay, but I also hope he learns something from this."

"Well—" I had no idea what to say.

Fortunately, she had something else on her mind. "Glen, you have to talk to Charlie."

"Huh?"

"He needs to understand that he can't keep doing this sort of thing."

"You want me to tell him not to race cars?"

"No, Glen. That he can't always have what he wants."

"Nicole, I don't think he'd listen to me."

"But Glen, you're his best friend."

"I'm not sure he sees it that way."

"But someone has to talk to him. If you won't, who will?"

"You could. After all, it's you he's trying to date."

"You think I should talk to him?"

"Look, I don't know what I think. I'm mad as can be at him for causing the accident in the first place, and then he goes and saves Phil's life, and—and somehow I feel sorry for him—don't ask me why!"

"He didn't cause the accident!"

"But Phil would never have thought of racing if Charlie hadn't dared him."

"And Phil isn't mature enough to say 'no' to a dare?"

"You don't know Charlie! He can make people do things. He always knows just what to say to get Phil mad."

"Oh, come on, Glen. Nobody makes anybody else lose his temper."

"Well, if anybody could it's Charlie."

"You make him sound like some kind of monster."

"Not a monster. But he's pretty cold-blooded. I don't think he cares about anybody except himself."

"But, Glen, he doesn't know God!"

"So what?"

"So he acts the way he does because he doesn't know any better."

"Before I knew God, I didn't go around trying to get people killed!"

"Charlie didn't intend Phil to crash!"

"But he made it happen!"

"He made Phil crash?" Her voice was skeptical.

"No, he didn't make him crash. But—"

"Phil needs to learn some self-control!"

"You don't know Phil very well."

"I've never wanted to know him well. Or Charlie, either," Nicole said. "But maybe it's time I do get to know them so I can judge for myself."

Being somewhat less than an expert on what to say to girls, I said, "Oh, come on."

She hurried into the school.

# 6

It looked as if Nicole and I had just had our first fight, if that's what you call it. Was this what going with a girl was like? If so, I wasn't sure I wanted any part of it.

Since I had no idea what else to do, I went to class and hoped she'd come to her senses.

Of course, everybody knew about the accident. As I went down the hall, that's all I heard kids talking about. A few asked me if I had heard anything more, but I shook my head and kept walking.

Marta Billings was standing near my locker. She was wearing black net stockings and a black skirt and a baggy black sweater. Oh, yeah, and black lipstick and nail polish. But what else was new?

As I opened my locker, she came close. "How's the love-life going?" she asked innocently.

Ignoring her, I started throwing things around in my locker. Where was my stupid science book, anyway?

"I hear Phil and Charlie were fighting over Nicole."

I looked up and said, "What?"

She shrugged her shoulders and swung her long black hair. "That's what I heard."

"Aren't you forgetting something?"

"What?"

"Nicole is going with me!"

Just then Nicole walked right by. I might have been invisible for all the notice she took of me.

"Yes, I can see that," Marta said sarcastically.

"Why don't you go and see if you can stuff yourself into the first aid kit," I said. "And while you're there, put a bandage over your mouth!" I walked past her into the classroom.

My immediate thought was how Jesus would be really proud of me for talking like that. For crying out loud, being a

Christian seemed to be making me worse instead of better! I'd never spoken to anyone like that before in my life! Not that I could remember, anyway. But surely, if God knew Marta, he would make an exception!

The two afternoon classes dragged on. Charlie wasn't there. I looked like an idiot several times when teachers asked me something and I didn't even hear the question, never mind knowing what the answer was. Of course, that wasn't entirely unusual for me.

Fortunately, the teachers seemed to understand my mind was elsewhere.

For that matter, a lot of kids weren't concentrating. After all, most of us had grown up together, so in a way we were kind of like a family. As for Marta and a few others—well, every family has its oddballs!

After classes, I talked to Mac and Brett—mostly speculating as to how Phil would cope if he really turned out to be paralyzed. Phil stuck in a wheel chair was one thing I didn't even want to picture.

Then I saw Nicole going to her locker and hurried after her. "I take it you're mad at me?" I asked.

She wasn't smiling. "I don't know."

"Me neither."

"What?"

"I don't know if you're mad at me."

"I'm not mad."

"You were."

"You always side with Phil."

"I don't. Actually, Phil's done some stupid things. But I don't think Charlie is blameless. That's all I said."

"You used to be Charlie's friend."

"I was Phil's friend first."

She looked steadily at me. Then she took a punch. Oh, not a real one—a verbal one. She said, "I thought I knew you. Now I'm not so sure I do."

There wasn't much I could say to that. I'd thought it too good to be true that Nicole wanted to date me, so it wasn't exactly a surprise to find she was having second thoughts. "Well," I said slowly. "I guess that's it, then. I'll see you around."

I got my stuff out of my locker and waved to Mac and Brett. They were going to Harry's for Cokes, but I had no desire to go with them.

Instead, I went home, walking the long way past the Grants' house, but taking care that no one saw me. I stood down the street for a minute and just stared at the house.

Finally, I went home and was glad to find a note from Mom that she had gone to see Mrs. Trent. I went into my room and shut the door. I pulled down the blind so it was dark and fell onto my stomach on the bed. If I'd been a girl, maybe I'd have burst into tears. But I'm not, and I don't think I could have cried even if I'd wanted to. Instead, I just lay there trying to remember if I'd ever felt worse.

After dinner, I asked Dad if I could take the car to the hospital. I wasn't sure they'd let me in to see Phil, but according to Mom he was out of intensive care, so I hoped they might.

As it turned out, Mrs. Trent was there and the nurse asked her if it was all right for me to see him. She said yes and the nurse gave me two minutes.

There were butterflies in my stomach as I pushed open the heavy door and went in. Phil was lying on a strange-looking bed with a bunch of tubes coming out of both arms and his nose. There were bandages on his head and more on his chest, and his face was still white.

But his eyes were open and he was watching me.

I grinned weakly, "Hi."

He responded with a grunt.

I went closer. "I'm glad you're doing okay," I said.

"Okay?" he whispered.

"Well," I said awkwardly, "I mean you're—well, you're alive."

"Thanks to Charlie."

"Yeah," I said, knowing how he must have felt when they told him Charlie had kept him from burning to death. "So, how long will they keep you here?" I asked, not knowing what else to say.

"Don't know."

"Is there anything I can get you?"

"No."

I looked around and saw flowers and magazines and fruit and a walkman and a TV. He seemed well-supplied. "Phil?"

"Yeah?"

"I'm—I'm real sorry this happened."

I could barely hear him. "I should have known I couldn't beat Charlie at anything. It's like he's surrounded by luck."

"Yeah. But, well, thanks. You got into it because you were trying to protect me."

"Oh?"

"Yeah."

"Well, I didn't. That was just an excuse to argue with Charlie. You know I've never liked him."

"No kidding."

"The only problem is," he complained, "he comes out on top every time."

"Yeah, I've noticed."

"His car could have flipped just as easily as mine. But no! It had to be me."

"Maybe it's time you and Charlie became friends," I said half-seriously.

"Yeah," he said. "Just what I always wanted."

I stood there awkwardly, wondering what to say that might help. "I hope you aren't thinking of doing anything to get even."

"Like this?" he asked bitterly. "From now on, I don't care what he does." His words were difficult to hear, and disjointed. "Maybe nearly getting killed makes you see what's important. Here I am flipping a car over and for what? Even you know that sooner or later Nicole is going to go out with Charlie. Everybody knows that."

What I would have found to say I don't know. Fortunately, a gray-haired nurse burst through the door and winked at me and said I'd have to go so she could look after Phil.

Grateful for her interruption, I escaped. I'm not even sure I said good-bye. I walked mechanically through the corridors to the front door and out to the parking lot, got in the car, and sat there.

So many thoughts were in my mind that it was impossible to actually think. I needed to be alone, and I knew if I went home it might be difficult. So I started the car and drove through town to the highway. I drove on it for about fifteen minutes, then turned onto a side road I knew. There was a bridge a little ways down. I parked the car off the road and made my way down the frozen bank to the small creek the bridge spanned. It wasn't easy walking along the frozen, stony ground in the dark, but I appreciated having to concentrate on the physical challenge. It took my mind off other things.

I walked for nearly two hours. I thought about Phil and what I could do to help. I thought about Nicole and me and Charlie, and how there was no telling what else Charlie would do to get Nicole. And now I wasn't sure Nicole even liked me any more. Then I thought about God and wondered if there was something more I should be doing now that I was a Christian. I felt frustrated by the fact that none of the kids from the church had been very friendly. Except Nicole and Joyce, of course. Shouldn't the others be glad I had become a Christian? Shouldn't they at least talk to me? There must be something I didn't understand.

I tried to clear my mind and just concentrate on walking and breathing deeply of the cool, fresh air.

When I got back to the car, I felt somewhat better. But there were just so many things happening. Since Charlie had moved into town, my life had been a constant whirl of things to worry about.

Speaking of whirling, Mom and Dad were just finishing moving things around in the basement when I got home. They asked about Phil and I repeated some of our conversation. Then I went upstairs and got some juice to drink. After that I went to my room and lay flat on the bed for a long time, feeling totally rotten. Memories of my conversation with Phil flooded my mind. Especially, I remembered his last words—how everybody knew that sooner or later Nicole would go out with Charlie. Was I really stupid, or was everybody else wrong?

I remembered Nicole's dislike of Phil and the concern she had expressed for Charlie. It was just possible "everybody" was right.

Mom was yelling my name, so I dragged myself off the bed and to the hall.

"Phone, Glen!"

I walked slowly to the kitchen. I didn't really want to talk to anybody.

"Hi, buddy," said Charlie's voice. "How's it going?"

I wanted to slam down the receiver or scream at him or something, but instead I just stood there.

"Glen? Are you there?"

"Yeah," I said at last. "I'm here."

"We need to talk, buddy. Got a minute?'

"There's nothing to talk about."

"Oh yes, there is. It's between you and me now. Phil's not around to protect you any more."

I finally found a vent for the anger I felt. "You—you—! He's in the hospital wondering if he'll ever walk again and all you can think about is yourself!"

"He chose to race me. It's not my fault he wasn't good enough."

"You louse! You don't even care."

"It wasn't my fault he crashed! And, after all, I did save his life, didn't I?"

There was no point arguing with him. He always won. "What do you want?" I said wearily.

"To talk to you about Nicole."

"Not now. I'm too tired." Anyway, after what had happened today, I wasn't sure he needed to talk to me about her.

"Tomorrow then. After school. We'll go for a drive."

"Yeah, sure," I said. There was no point arguing. And right now I didn't care. As far as I knew, Nicole had already decided I wasn't worth her time. So what did it matter?

The next day I got through classes somehow. Every time I saw Nicole, she was busy talking to Joyce or Darlene or one of the other girls. She seemed to be avoiding me. Until school was over and I was at my locker.

"Glen."

I spun around.

"I guess we need to talk," she said softly.

"Yeah, I guess."

"Glen, I'm sorry I got upset and said what I did. Especially about Phil. I feel like an idiot. It was stupid for me to say those things—especially now when he's hurt." Tears were streaming down her cheeks. "Can you forgive me? I don't know why I said what I did."

Without thinking, I held out my arms and she came toward me and buried her face on my shoulder. Gingerly, I put my arms around her. I'm sure there were kids gawking at us, but I didn't care.

She was okay in a couple of minutes, and I told her that of course I would forgive her and that I knew we were both worried about Phil.

We were doing okay until I saw Charlie standing a few feet down the hall, leaning against a locker staring at us. He looked like he wanted to kill me.

I didn't want him to start something in front of Nicole. "Uh, I—uh, I guess I have to go," I said to her. "I—uh—sort of have an appointment."

She looked puzzled.

"Can I call you later?" I asked.

She nodded.

I walked over to Charlie. "Well, let's get this over with," I said, half-hoping he would punch me right there in the hallway.

But he turned without a word, and I followed him out of the school to his Mustang.

He got in the driver's side and when I didn't get in right away, he leaned over to open the passenger door and snarl, "Get in."

Wishing I could ignore him, I opened the door and sank into the bucket seat.

"So," he said as he started the car and drove out of the schoolgrounds, "were you having a nice time?" He didn't shout or anything, but I knew he was seething.

Not knowing what to say, I kept quiet.

"What on earth does she see in you?" Charlie asked. Although he didn't shout, each word had electricity crackling through it.

"I'm afraid I can't answer that," I said, "on the grounds that I might incriminate myself."

"Sauten, you can't even make a decent joke."

I didn't bother to reply.

"Phil I might understand—but you!" he said in disgust.

Since Phil had said something similar, I felt justifiably annoyed. But I still chose not to say anything.

"You aren't much of a friend," he said after a minute. "You knew I wanted Nicole, but you still went after her the moment my back was turned."

"Only when I found out it was me she liked."

"And how about the way you've acted? Not exactly friendly."

"Sorry, Charlie. You see, I had this guy trying to horn in on me and my girl. What else could I do?"

He digested that one for a minute. When he spoke again, he still had his anger under control. "You know as well as I do that you aren't good enough for her. On a scale of one to ten, you're a two and I'm a ten. Now—"

"I suppose Nicole's a ten," I said.

"Right. So—"

"So you and she deserve each other?"

"If you want to put it so crudely. You could say we were meant for each other."

"What if your scale is wrong?"

"It isn't."

"Yeah, but somebody else might have a different scale. Like God."

"God's got nothing to do with this!"

"Yes, he does."

"Only because Nicole's dad won't let her date me because I don't buy all that God talk."

"Well, I wasn't thinking about that. I was thinking about God's scale. The way I understand, his scale just has two points—zero and a hundred. Right now you're a zero and Nicole, Joyce and I are all hundreds. So you'd better think about that!"

He didn't say anything.

He had driven through town at only a little above the speed limit. Now that we were outside of town, he gunned it and I checked to make sure I had my seat belt on. I knew he was a good driver, but still—

"What she sees in a wimp like you, I'll never know."

"Charlie, slow down!"

"You're nothing but a chicken!"

I was getting awfully tired of being called that, but there was no point arguing. "Fine, I'm a chicken."

We drove along in silence for about five minutes. He kept going faster and faster. I started praying that God would look after us. Finally, I said, "Charlie, slow down."

"Tell me you'll leave Nicole alone and I'll slow down!"

"Never!"

"You don't have Phil around to protect you any more!"

"Beat me up if you want to," I shouted recklessly. "It won't make any difference."

The speedometer needle went higher.

"Slow down, you idiot!" I yelled. "Wasn't the accident yesterday enough for you?"

"Give me Nicole!"

I saw something black on the road ahead. I yelled, "Charlie, watch out!" And then I shut my eyes.

Tires squealed as he hit the brakes, swerving to avoid whatever was on the road. The car started rocking crazily from side to side, and for several tense moments I expected us to crash into the ditch. When we didn't, I opened my eyes and saw Charlie gripping the wheel, teeth clenched as he grimly fought for control. He won, and we stayed on the road, going slower. But as soon as the car was under control again, he began to pick up speed.

"Stop!" I yelled. "I think you hit something."

"It was only a stinking skunk!"

"Turn back!"

"No."

"Then stop! Let me out!"

He hit the brakes hard and we swung to a screeching halt on the shoulder.

"You should go back," I said quietly.

"You want to go back, get out. Otherwise, shut up."

I got out, and he yelled at me, "You'll have a long walk back to town. You can use it to think about what you're going to do. Nicole is the perfect girl for me. You'll regret it if you get in my way."

Then he tore off.

I had to walk a long way before I found the skid marks from the tires.

Even then, it took me several minutes to find the animal. I was beginning to think Charlie was right and I was an idiot for coming back. Besides, I was already nearly frozen, it was starting to get dark, and I was a long way from town.

I was about ready to give up when I heard a sharp high-pitched bark. Out of the corner of my eye, I saw something move against the dirty white snow in the ditch.

As I peered closer, I realized it was a small black and white dog of uncertain ancestry. It was lying on its side, head raised, black eyes watching me.

Hesitantly, I started down the bank toward it, my running shoes sliding on the hard-packed snow. I could see the dog more clearly now. It looked as if it was trying to get up, but it couldn't.

As I got closer, I saw the dog's fur was matted and dirty, and it looked thin and uncared for. It barked several times and feebly wagged its stump of a tail.

"Here, boy," I said softly. "It's okay. Come here."

Again, it tried to raise itself, but the back end seemed glued to the ground. The dog lay back, exhausted. Then it whimpered.

I've heard that even a pet will bite you if it's injured, so I was afraid to get too close. I went up to about three feet, and tried to see the back end. There was blood on the snow and on the dog's leg. So Charlie had hit it. Not more than a glancing touch, or the dog would have been dead.

Realizing I wasn't helping the dog by standing there, I took off my heavy jacket and rolled it around my right forearm. I had gloves on, so I thought I'd be safe. I came close, making sure my right arm was nearest the dog's head. But instead of trying to bite me, the dog tried to lick my hand.

Ashamed, I put the jacket down and patted the dog's head. It whimpered. I tried to see his back end. There didn't seem to be a lot of blood, but I did see a deep gash in the right leg, with what looked like bone sticking out. When I saw that, I felt like throwing up. But I gritted my teeth and carefully slid my jacket under the dog to make a kind of stretcher. He whimpered once more, and moaned a couple of times, but he made no attempt to bite me. In fact, he seemed barely able to lift his head.

Those big black eyes were open, though, and the dog's look seemed to say it trusted me to help.

"I don't know, boy," I said. "If you've got internal injuries, you'll likely be dead soon. There's no way I can carry you all the way back to town. Plus I'd freeze before we got there. So we better pray that somebody comes to give us a ride."

Gingerly, I wrapped the jacket securely around the dog and then picked up the bundle of jacket and dog as gently as I could. I was careful to keep one arm under the dog's back end, trying not to let that injured leg move any more than was absolutely necessary. I had had some practice carrying my nephews and nieces when they were babies, so I was able to do a reasonably good job.

I walked along the ditch until I found a place that was a little lower than where I'd come down. Soon I was walking along the road in just below freezing weather wearing a short-sleeved T-shirt, jeans, running shoes, and gloves, and carrying a winter jacket with a nearly dead dog in it. Great sight.

I couldn't see any farm houses, and I had no idea where the first one would be. I started talking out loud to God.

"I sure could use some help here, Lord. I mean, I need a lot of help. But right now, if you want this dog to survive, you had better do something. I know I can't do any more. I'm likely going to get pneumonia as it is. So please, if you aren't too busy, could you help out? But I'll understand if you don't have time. I mean, you must have lots more important things to do. Like Phil. Lord, could you please do something about Phil? I know he's more important than a dog. But I don't know how to help him, either!"

I had tears coming to my eyes by now, some from my thoughts and some from the cold. But I kept going, walking and praying, and hoping God really would do something.

I heard a motor behind me and turned just in time to see a brown minivan go speeding by. It made no attempt to stop.

People are like that sometimes. They walk right by without even seeming to notice you. I wonder if they don't care or if they're just too busy with their own thoughts.

"Thanks a lot, God," I said. Immediately I felt ashamed. It wasn't his fault the van hadn't stopped. The person driving the van had made that choice.

I heard another motor, and I turned again. It was the tow truck from Winter's Garage, pulling a car behind it. As the truck went past, my heart sank.

# 7

But as it went by, I realized the truck was slowing down. "Thank You, God," I whispered.

It stopped about fifty feet down the road and John Hamilton jumped out and hurried back to me. "Glen?" he shouted in surprise. "Is that you? What are you doing out here? And why aren't you wearing your coat?"

I hurried toward him. "Injured dog. Needs a vet."

He didn't waste any words either. Just a quick, "Get in," as he opened the door and basically lifted me into the cab of the truck. He ran around to the other side, jumped in, and grabbed a blanket from behind his seat to throw around my shoulders.

As he shifted gears and got the truck moving, he asked, "What happened? Where's your car?"

"It's a long story," I said. To my surprise, I found myself telling him everything—all about Nicole and Charlie and Phil and how I'd managed to get myself in the situation he had found me in.

He was a good listener, and he didn't laugh once.

John didn't need directions because the vet's office was a little over block down Main Street from Winter's Garage.

We pulled up in front just as I was finishing my story, so he didn't have time to comment.

He jumped out of the cab, at the same time saying, "Stay put till I make sure he's here."

The door was unlocked, so he came back and helped me out. I had opened the jacket up in the truck so I could see the dog's head and tell if he was still breathing. He was, but he was also very limp.

There was no one in the small waiting room, but we could hear voices from behind a closed door. Hesitantly, John rapped.

Footsteps approached; then the door opened and Dr. Clifton, a small wiry man with a brownish-gray mustache, poked his head out.

"I found a dog," I said stupidly.

"Sorry, I don't look after lost animals." He started to shut the door.

"No," I yelled. "He's injured."

The door opened a bit wider. "How badly?" he asked.

"I think his leg's broken, and there could be more."

He sighed. "Well, I'll have a look at him, but this isn't a charity, you know."

"I'll pay for it," I said impulsively.

His eyebrows went up. "Do you have any idea whose dog it is?"

I shook my head. "Maybe you'll recognize him?" I asked hopefully.

He shut the door behind him. "Where is he?"

"In here," I held my arms out.

He lifted his eyebrows again as he took in my T-shirt and the jacket in my arms. "Follow me," he said, and we went through another door.

Carefully, I set my bundle down on a stainless steel table. With trembling hands, I opened the jacket and revealed the small black and white dog lying on its side. His eyes were shut but as if realizing we were watching, the dog opened them and feebly wagged his tail once.

Dr. Clifton said nothing. He listened to the dog's heartbeat, and ran his hands over the thin body. When he came near the leg, he shook his head. He touched it very gently. The dog whimpered.

Doctor Clifton walked out of the room and John and I followed. He went to a filing cabinet in the front and pulled out a file folder.

"The dog's name is Scruffy," he said. "He's four years old, and he belongs to a family named Hicks. They were living on a farm west of here. About two weeks ago, Mr. Hicks brought the dog in and asked me to put him down."

"You mean kill him?" I asked.

"If you want to call it that, yes."

"But why?"

"They were moving in with Mr. Hicks' in-laws in the city, and there was no room for the dog. He said his wife had asked around and no one wanted it. It was his little girl's dog."

"But—"

"When I told him how much I would charge, he said he wasn't throwing away money he didn't have just to get rid of a dog."

"So he moved and left the dog?" I asked.

"Apparently."

"How could he have survived the cold?"

"Dogs are smart. He could get into a barn and bury himself in the hay. This one has a fairly thick coat, too."

"Can you help him?"

"I'm not sure. He's run down, even without the injury. Do you know what happened?"

"He was near the road. Likely got clipped by a passing car." I wasn't going to blame Charlie. It wasn't his fault the dog was loose.

"If I do operate on the dog, it would be expensive. Kinder to put him out of his suffering. After all, he has no home."

"He does now," I said without thinking.

"You have the money?" It was obvious he didn't think so.

"I have over two thousand dollars in the bank," I replied. "And I can get a job if I need more."

He smiled for the first time. "I don't think it will cost that much."

He walked back into the examining room where the dog lay helplessly on my jacket. His eyes were closed, but when I put my hand out to touch his nose, that little pink tongue pushed out and made a half-hearted attempt to lick my hand.

Maybe Mr. Hicks hadn't liked the dog much, but somebody had taught it to trust people.

"Well, you two better get out of here and let me see what I can do. No guarantees, mind. He's not in good shape and I could lose him."

"But you will do your best?" I asked.

He peered over his glasses at me. "You look familiar. Who's your dad?"

"Matthew Sauten."

"Oh, of course. Knew you reminded me of someone."

He paused, absently looking around the room. "Well, get out," he said suddenly, as if just remembering we were still around.

"What about your jacket?" John asked.

I picked it up, but didn't put it on. The inside was a mess.

We went to the truck and John drove me home. We were pretty quiet until John said, "Well, I'm impressed."

I looked at him, wondering what he was talking about.

"You handled that very well."

"I did?"

"Wouldn't you say so?"

I shrugged. "I don't know. I just, well, I just wanted to make sure the dog got looked after."

"And you did. Now, if the vet is successful, are your parents going to agree with you about having a dog?"

I blew out my breath. "Who knows?"

"Would you like to stop and pray about it?"

I was surprised, but I guess I shouldn't have been. After all, this was the guy who talked to God out loud during lunch.

So we stopped and prayed. And when he prayed, wow! He remembered everything I'd told him about Phil and Nicole and Charlie, and he not only prayed for Scruffy—what a dumb name—but for me and Phil and everybody. He really prayed. I mean, not just saying "Please help Phil," but praying like he knew God was right in the truck with us and was just waiting for us to indicate what needed to be done.

Which reminded me of something. When he was finished, I said, "By the way, back there on the road, I was praying like crazy that God would send help. Then you came along."

He smiled. "Don't sound so surprised."

"Well, lately, everything's been going wrong and I've been feeling pretty much alone. I guess I was kind of surprised to see you."

"Just remember, when you ask God to work in your life, he doesn't always do things the way you expect. Sometimes he allows things to happen which we consider bad but he considers good because of the result. Know what I mean?"

"I guess." I know I didn't sound very confident.

"Well, take me for instance. I really didn't want to move to this town. Not that there's anything wrong with the town; it just wasn't what I wanted. But I got laid off from my job a while ago and I couldn't find anything else to do, so when I heard about this job, I knew I had to apply. I asked God to close the door if he didn't want us here, and I have to admit I hoped he would close it. But he left it wide open. So you see, the reason I was out on that road today to help you was because I got laid off and went without a decent job for four months. Think about it, Glen. God must love you a whole lot to do all that to get me here so I could help you take that dog to a vet."

What do you say to someone with logic like that?

He drove to my house and stopped the truck, and laughed when I got out. I guess I still looked as stunned as I felt. "Talk to you later," he called as he drove off.

I realized I hadn't even once thanked him.

There was no one home, so I grabbed some hot chocolate, turned on a loud cops and robbers show, and sank onto the chesterfield with an afghan on top of me. For about twenty minutes, I sat there shivering from the chill I'd had, feeling dumb for not thanking John, and trying to figure out how to convince my parents we needed an injured dog.

I heard the door.

"Glen, are you here?" asked my mom's voice.

"Yeah."

"Guess what?" She appeared to float into the room. "I've got a job!"

I groaned and stretched full out on the chesterfield.

"I can't believe it—" she went on, totally oblivious to my condition "—but I was talking to Joanne Weston the other day and she said I should ask at the school, and so I thought, why not? So I did, and Phyllis Marshall is taking a leave of absence to have a baby, and they hired me! And they say if it works out, they'll need me for next year because Mrs. Simpson is planning to retire at the end of the school year! And the hours are really good! I'll be home in time to get dinner and visit with you. I'll be around kids, which you know I like. Isn't it great! I was so excited I went straight to the bank to tell your dad, and he thought it was wonderful! We're going to eat out tonight to celebrate! Your dad will be here in a few minutes, so get ready. I'm going to change."

She whirled out of the room and I just lay there.

Then she came back. "Glen," she said in an uncertain voice, "are you okay? You aren't feeling sick are you? Are you worried about Phil?"

"I'm fine, Mom," I managed to get out. "Just a little tired."

"You—you aren't sorry I got this job are you?"

"No, Mom, it's great." I tried to smile, but it's a tossup as to whether it was a smile or a grimace. Fortunately, Mom was too caught up with the new job to notice.

"I hope you don't mind my being at the school."

"'Course not," I assured her. But I started wondering what she was talking about. At the school? Mrs. Simpson? I sat up. "Uh, Mom?"

"Yes, Glen?"

"Would you mind repeating that bit about where you got a job?"

"At the school. I'll be working in the office. As a receptionist for now."

"At the *high* school?"

"Yes, at the high school."

I fell back onto the chesterfield. My mom had a job in the office at the high school. That was all I needed. And any minute Dad would be home and I would have to go out with them to celebrate.

"Glen?" Mom asked. "Is it a problem? If you'd rather I didn't take the job—"

"No, no," I fibbed. "It sounds great. You'll like it."

"You're sure you don't mind?"

I gritted my teeth. "Mind? Why should I mind?"

She came closer and gave me a hug. "I knew you'd be okay with it. You're so mature these days." She stood up. "Well, let's get ready to go out! We'll stop at the hospital afterwards. I talked to Phil's mom and he's much better. The doctor says he's in really good shape physically, and that helps."

She went to her room and I lay on the couch for a couple more minutes before I could muster enough energy to lift myself up. Somehow, I dragged myself to my room. I sat on the edge of the bed and looked around. I knew I should put on some different clothes. Mom might not say anything if I didn't, but she would notice.

I looked around, wishing my fairy godmother or maybe godfather would pop up and make all the decisions for me. But of course that only happens in fairy tales.

However, while I was looking around, I spotted my Bible. It was on the bottom of a pile of junk on my desk.

A stab of guilt went through me as I realized I hadn't read my Bible since school started. When I first got it, I had read it every day. But lately I'd been so busy with everything that I guess I'd just forgotten about it.

Maybe it wasn't surprising that I felt so all alone. Maybe God was just waiting to tell me what to do and here I was not even bothering to see what he had to say!

"Are you almost ready, Glen?" asked Mom's voice from the hall. "Your dad just drove up."

"Be right there, Mom," I yelled. "I'll read you later," I said to my Bible. To make sure I didn't forget, I got it out from under the other stuff and put it on my pillow. I pulled on a pair of clean pants and, still buttoning my shirt, hurried out to the kitchen.

Dad was there, and I could tell he was really pleased about Mom's job. I forced a smile onto my face.

"Well, Glen, how about it? Think your mom will like working there?"

"Uh, yeah, sure, Dad. It's okay."

"Hey, maybe you can go to school together in the morning!" He laughed and I knew he knew what I was thinking.

"Don't tease him, Matt. You know he's not going to enjoy having his mother there knowing every time he gets a detention."

"I don't get detentions," I protested. "Except maybe for being late."

"Then I guess you'd better not go to school together," laughed Dad, "or you'll both get detentions."

"That would be carrying togetherness a little too far," Mom said.

"Is anybody else hungry?" I asked.

We went out to the car and that's when Mom noticed I was wearing an old jacket that I'd found in the basement. Remembering the blood on my good jacket, I said something about its needing cleaning, and saw Mom give Dad a funny look. But she didn't say any more. Soon we were at the hotel, which has the only sort of fancy restaurant in town. We ordered, and then I kind of sat and mulled over my life while Dad and Mom chatted with a couple of people they knew at the next table.

After a while the food came and we were all busy eating. I tried to keep up with what was going on so I wouldn't look like a dope if either of them asked me something, and I guess I managed okay. At least, neither of them asked me what was wrong. I guess they assumed I was thinking about Phil.

We had chocolate cheesecake for dessert, and then we stopped at the hospital. We saw Phil, but only for a few minutes, and because my parents were along, I didn't have to actually talk to him.

He looked pretty down, and barely said anything. His mom did most of the talking—about how he was getting better every day, and what the nurses were like, and the hospital food and other stuff.

I told him I'd be over tomorrow, and we went home.

One of Mom and Dad's favorite shows was on TV, so they sat down to watch it and I went to my room. I didn't have any homework to worry about—not that I would have worried about it anyway. But I didn't, so I settled down on the bed to read my Bible. I just started leafing through from the front, as if I were hoping God would suddenly shout out, "There it is! That's the page I want you to read!"

And the funny thing is, he did. At least, he didn't shout anything out, but as I was leafing through, the writing near the top of one page caught my attention. It said "A Psalm of Complaint and of Praise." I guess I noticed it for two reasons; one was that I felt like complaining to somebody about all the things that were making my life miserable; the other was that it sounded odd to put complaining beside praising. How could you do both at the same time?

Anyway, I stopped and looked at the psalm, which was number thirty-one, and then I noticed it was written by King David. That must be the guy Nicole had told me about—the one who had been a great king. But he'd been something else—what had she said? "A man after God's own heart."

That meant God was happy with him. So what did he have to complain about?

I decided to read it. Then I read it again. It seemed David was having problems. He said he was getting old and had lost his strength and all his friends. People crossed the street to avoid meeting him. He even had enemies trying to kill him. But he wasn't worried, because God was with him. He believed God would not only take care of him but also shame his enemies. What I really liked was the last bit, where it said, "Be strong and let your heart take courage, all you who hope in the Lord."

It was as if David were right there talking to me and saying, "Look, Glen, it doesn't matter that Charlie wants to steal your girl, or that Phil seems mad at you, and it doesn't even matter if you lose Nicole; all that matters is that God loves you and he'll see you through this."

Right then I felt a lot better. But I also felt ashamed of the way I'd treated God the last week. I shut my eyes and asked him to forgive me for ignoring him, and promised to try harder in the future and not get caught up in things that weren't as important in the long run—even schoolwork.

I felt bad about how I'd reacted to Mom's job news, so I went out and told her I really was happy about her getting the job, and I said I was going to bed to make sure I didn't get a detention for being late the next day.

I didn't have a single dream that night. And I still felt fairly good the next morning. Mom was up and ready, but without saying anything, she just left, walking by herself. I left earlier than usual myself.

I saw Nicole in the hallway with Joyce. She said, "Hello, Glen," and kept going.

It was at that point I remembered that when I'd talked to her after school yesterday, I'd promised to phone her last night. I'd blown it again.

I raced after her. "Nicole, wait up!"

"Did you want something, Glen?" Her voice was cold.

"I forgot to phone you!"

"That's okay. You can't remember everything you promise."

She would have turned and walked away, but I grabbed her arm. "Nicole, I'm sorry. Something important came up."

She looked at me, her eyes open wide. "I guess I'm not very important." Her voice and look were both very dignified, but the effect was somewhat spoiled by Joyce, who giggled.

"Of course, you're important," I said. "But this was—well, you have to let me explain." But explain what? About Charlie trying to convince me to let him have her? Or his speeding to scare me? Would she believe me? And did I tell her about his hitting the dog?

Nicole was impatient. "Well, you said you wanted to explain?"

"I—uh, well—"

"I saw you leave with Charlie, who I thought you said you weren't so friendly with these days."

"I'm not, but he wanted to talk about—uh, about—"

"Yes?"

"Phil. He wanted to talk about Phil."

Her voice softened. "Oh, that's different. Did you patch things up?"

"Well, not exactly. But then I found this dog. It was hurt, so I took it to the vet. Then Mom got a job and we had to go out and celebrate. I never had a chance to call you. Honest."

"Where'd you find the dog, Glen?" Joyce asked.

"Out in the country. In a ditch. It had been hit by a car." I kept talking, knowing that the more I said, the less time they would have to think of more questions.

"Is it okay?" Joyce appeared to be the one interested in the dog.

But I knew Nicole was listening.

I kept my eyes on Joyce. "I don't know. I called this morning, but there was only an answering machine. I'll call between classes and maybe go over there at lunch."

"Whose dog is it?"

"Somebody who moved away and just left it alone."

"How could anybody do that?" Nicole asked, her eyes round with amazement.

"Lots of people do nasty things," I said. "Sometimes without realizing it." I thought of Charlie. Did he realize what he was doing all the time?

The bell rang, and I avoided having to answer any more questions. As I sat in my desk for first class, I took a deep breath and exhaled slowly.

This girl-guy stuff was more complicated than I'd thought. How come Phil and Charlie never seemed to have problems like this? Or, wait a minute–maybe they did. After all, look at how Lisa had treated Phil. And Charlie had been nearly turning inside out to get Nicole to like him. The real question should be, what keeps them going back for more?

Speaking of Charlie, he was back at school, acting as if nothing had happened. You know, real polite to the teachers, always ready with the right answers, overly nice to the girls, and buddy-buddy with the guys.

Only most of the kids had known Phil all their lives, so I got the impression Charlie's show of everything's being okay wasn't going far. They talked to him, but they weren't all that friendly. I even saw a couple turn their backs on him. Which seemed to make him try all the harder.

There was a strange teacher in homeroom. I wondered where Mr. Jackman was. But I didn't have long to wonder. The man waited for us all to sit down and then announced, "I'm Mr. Reynolds. I'll be teaching Mr. Jackman's classes for the next few weeks. His son is very ill, and Mr. and Mrs. Jackman have gone to be with him. Now, open your texts to page one hundred eighty-three."

I opened my book, but all I could think about was Mr. Jackman's son, Frank. We'd known he was sick, and that he hadn't been given long to live. But now—well, it was here. I wondered how they were taking it. There was one other son, too. Frank was the elder—about twenty-five or six. He wasn't married, but he'd been working in a city quite far away since he went to college, and he hadn't been home much. Now he was dying and there was nothing anybody could do to help him. Mr. Jackman was the strictest teacher I'd ever had, and I wasn't real crazy about him, but you still had to wonder how he was doing watching his own son die like that.

We got through the class, but I don't remember much of what went on. We had to read a chapter and answer questions in the book—the kind of stuff a substitute teacher gives.

I called Dr. Clifton between first and second class. He said there was no point in my coming over before school was out. He wasn't sure there was any point in my coming then, either, but he didn't say I couldn't.

I looked for Nicole, but she must have already gone home for lunch. I figured she'd be upset about Mr. Jackman. She's sensitive, and she really cares about people—even a grumpy teacher. I wanted to say something to her—like I understood how she felt, but I didn't see her. So I walked home myself and wished there was some way you could just go into a nice little cocoon and forget about all the bad things that are going on—all the people dying, whether from illness or in wars or whatever, and all the murders and cruelty and hunger. But I guess there isn't any way, not unless you turn to drugs or alcohol or something like that. But they don't solve any of the problems. When you come back to earth, the situations are just the same, or maybe worse. And you're hurting yourself, too.

It's tough.

I thought of the verses I'd read last night about David and how alone he'd felt. Maybe everybody feels alone sometimes. Maybe Mr. Jackman felt like that right now. But what could somebody like me do to help?

For some reason, I thought of John Hamilton, and I just started praying. I didn't shut my eyes, of course, because I didn't want to trip over something.

I got home and made a peanut butter sandwich. It seemed funny for Mom not to be there. She had taken her lunch because she had to work for part of the lunch hour.

I ate slowly, thinking about what I was going to say to Phil when I saw him. What do you say to a friend who may be paralyzed? And what about Charlie? I couldn't spend the rest of the year avoiding him. What did God expect me to do?

Something difficult, no doubt.

I decided to pull out my Bible and read it. Wouldn't you know, I opened it to a page about David. Only he wasn't a king then. I vaguely remembered Nicole's saying something about this, but I didn't remember the story. David was just a boy, bringing food to his older brothers, who were soldiers. David got real angry because nobody in the army, including his brothers, would go out to fight this big guy, Goliath. So

David fought him, without armor or anything except a few stones and his sling. Because God was on his side, he won.

I thought about that as I walked back to school. And about what John had said. How God doesn't always do what we expect. Who would have thought a boy could defeat Goliath? Maybe Phil's being paralyzed was all tied up in the way Phil would come to know God.

But somebody still had to tell him.

The first people I saw as I came up to the school were Andy and Derek, who both went to church and the youth group. They just looked at me, neither angry nor friendly, and I lost my temper. Me! I went back to them and said, "For guys who are supposed to be Christians, you sure aren't doing much to help!"

# 8

I left the two of them standing there looking totally stunned. I couldn't believe what I'd said, but I sure wasn't going back to try to explain.

Nicole was at her locker when I reached it.

"I'm going to see Phil last period," I said. "I have a spare. How about you?"

"I have a class," she said. She turned slowly toward me. "Glen, I've been thinking about this and I think there's something I should tell you. About Phil." She looked away. "You see, I've never really liked him and I've often wished you wouldn't hang around with him so much. And—"

I'd always thought she liked everybody. "You don't like Phil?" I asked in surprise. "Why?"

"Oh—" she laughed nervously "—he always looks so sloppy and acts so careless, and I know he drinks now and then and goes to dances and movies all the time. And he's dated a lot of girls and—oh, you know. He acts so—*macho* is the word, I guess. He reminds me of a rebel who doesn't care about what's right or wrong."

"So that's why you got mad when I stood up for him!"

She nodded. "The truth is I was really glad when Charlie moved here and you started coming to church with him and you even seemed to pay more attention to how you looked and everything. It was great!

"Only now things are so mixed up. You still seem to like Phil better than Charlie, and, well, I don't know what to think. Especially now. I mean, I don't want to be unfair to Phil while he's hurt."

"So you *do* like Charlie!"

"I like some things about him. He always looks—well, like he cares about how he looks. But don't get me wrong. I know that what's important is what's inside. But he is smart, and polite, and—well, I think he just needs to know God and he'd be a really nice guy."

"You could be right about Charlie. I don't know. But you're wrong about Phil. He's not what you think. I'd rather have Phil than anybody else. Except you, of course," I added hastily.

"I know you believe that. I guess that's what I'm having trouble with, really. Wondering if—this sounds dumb—if you know what you're doing. About Phil and Charlie, I mean."

I saw her point. She wasn't sure whether she could trust my judgment. Well, not many people would. So I couldn't very well blame her for wondering.

"Are you mad at me?" she asked.

"No, I'm not mad."

"What then?"

"I don't know."

She looked up at me but didn't say anything.

I shrugged. "I was just thinking, I guess. About life, and how hard it is to figure out what's going to happen next."

"Nobody knows the future," she said.

"Yeah."

"We're probably better off not knowing. The Bible says that there is enough trouble in the day itself without worrying about tomorrow."

"Yeah, I guess."

I told her she could come with me to see Phil sometime if she wanted, but that it didn't matter.

"I'll think about it, Glen. I hope you aren't upset with me. I hope the dog gets better, too."

"Thanks," I said. "I'll talk to you later."

She left and I hurried to my locker to pick up the books I needed for my class. Who should be there but Marta.

"Hi, Glen," she said in this syrupy sweet voice. She was leaning against the locker next to mine, her hands behind her back.

I looked at her warily. "What do you want?"

"Just this!" She brought her hands out from behind her back. She had something that looked like a pen, and the next thing I knew she was squirting ink all over my shirt. "Bye!" she called as she took off down the hall, laughing.

I could hear snickers from other kids. But all I could do was stand there saying, "Why me?"

As it turned out, it was some strange kind of ink that disappeared in a few minutes, so there was no permanent damage. I guess I deserved it after the way I had talked to her on Monday. But I sure wished she'd grow up and act her age.

A little over an hour later, at the hospital, I had to wait because Phil already had a visitor—Lisa. When she came out and saw me, she just said, "Next."

I stood up.

"Sorry," she said. "Seeing him like that makes me—I don't know. I hate it. I hate coming here and I hate seeing him that way. I don't even know why I bother to come. It's not as if he wants to see me." She stalked off.

He still had several tubes in him, but this time the bed was somehow on top of him. He was upside down, strapped on so he didn't fall. When I stood there staring, he told me to come in. He could see me in a mirror that was set at an angle in front of this eyes.

He said it was called a Stryker bed and they flipped it every once in a while so he didn't get too uncomfortable from being in one position all the time.

"How are you doing?" I asked stupidly.

"I'm wishing people wouldn't ask me that. It's very boring to have to answer the same question over and over."

"I saw Lisa coming out."

"Yeah, she came by. Even brought me some flowers and a book. Oh, yeah, she also told me she isn't going out with Charlie any more–and she said Charlie and I are both idiots."

There was a long pause, with neither of us knowing what to say. Finally, I asked how he liked his nurses and we talked about hospitals for a while. Phil had a few funny stories about how they wake you up to give you sleeping pills and stuff like that. We were still talking when his mom and dad came in. "Oh, Glen," his mom said. "It's good to see you here."

I got up to go, but she told me to stay and they would get coffee and come back later. "I'm sure he'd rather talk to you than us," she said.

I sat back down, but then there was an awkward silence. I knew I had to say something. I took a deep breath and said, "Phil, uh, is it really true?"

"Is what true?"

"That you—uh—don't—uh, you know—feel anything?"

"You mean am I paralyzed?" he asked harshly.

"Yeah."

"I don't feel a thing in my legs. There's a good chance I never will."

"How—how are you doing?"

"Oh, I'm having a great time. What do you think?"

"I just wanted to—you know—to tell you—"

"What?"

"Well—" I tried to get comfortable in the chair "—well, uh, that I'm praying for you." The words were out at last.

"Yeah, I'm sure that'll help." His tone was sarcastic.

Without realizing I was doing it, I stood up and started walking around. I was glad he had a private room so nobody else had to listen to my fumbling. "Phil," I said, "I don't know if I've changed or not on the outside, but I do know that I've changed inside. I know God is real. He cares about me and about you and even about Charlie. He wants us to care about each other, too. I'm not very good at this, but I have to try to tell you. If your legs really are paralyzed, that will be terrible, but it will be even worse if you don't know God, because then you're paralyzed inside."

He didn't interrupt me, and since he was more or less a captive audience, I kept going. I told him about David and how God had helped him defeat Goliath, and I told him how God could help him overcome paralysis if it turned out that he really couldn't walk again. I even opened my Bible, which I had brought, and read part of Psalm 31. I finished by telling him how Jesus had died for us because we couldn't get close to God any other way, and how all he had to do was ask Jesus into his life and he could become a new person inside, too.

When I was finished, I glanced over at him.

"You through?" he said.

"Yes."

"Good. Now get out."

"What?"

"Get out." His voice was calm, but it was like granite. "If there is a God, which I seriously doubt, why would he let something like this happen? Don't try to tell me he loves me. Is this how you show love?"

"But he does, Phil!"

"Glen?"

"Yeah?"

"How long have we been friends?"

"I don't know. Since we were four or five, I guess."

"Well, if you want to stay friends, I don't want you to talk to me about God again. Not ever, you hear? Just because you got brainwashed by Nicole and her dad doesn't mean you have to go passing it around to everybody else."

"But it's real, Phil."

"Look," he said evenly, "if I could get up, I'd throw you out, but since I can't, I'm telling you. I don't want to hear any more about it. I'll find some way to get even with you if you say any more." He still hadn't raised his voice, but I knew he was dead serious. "Now get out."

I did as requested, passing his parents in the hall as I went.

When I got outside, I found a bench and slumped onto it. I had been so sure that God wanted me to talk to Phil. And now—! "God, what do you want from me?" I demanded. "He didn't hear a word I said. Why did you let me make such a fool of myself?" Tears of frustration burned my eyes, and I wanted to sink right through the wooden seat and never have to face anyone again.

I was halfway home when I remembered the dog. I had told Dr. Clifton I'd drop by after school. So I turned and headed back to Main Street and his office.

On the way, I passed Winter's Garage. Remembering that I hadn't thanked John for helping me out yesterday, I decided to drop in. He was in the office, taking a check from Mr. Billings, Marta's dad.

My first impulse on seeing Mr. Billings was to ask him how he came to have such an idiotic daughter, but I resisted. Actually, I don't think much of him, either. He's a salesman for some candy company and he travels a lot. Taking orders, I guess. He has the same black hair as Marta, cut short but not too short, and sort of greasy-looking. I guess he puts something on it to keep it flat. Unlike Marta, he's overweight, as if he samples those candies a lot. And he's sort of—oh, too friendly, I guess. It's hard to describe, but I've never liked him —even as a little kid when he occasionally came to school and gave out candies. There's something about the look in his eyes, which seems to be hard, in contrast to his ready smile. I always felt like he was somehow bribing us with the candy.

Anyway, he was arguing with John over the bill, so I waited, listening as John patiently explained why the charges were what they were and kept his cool when Mr. Billings more or less accused him of padding the bill. He didn't quite come out and say anything racial, but you could feel the possibility in the air. Finally, realizing John wasn't going to argue with him or give in, he paid it and left.

John turned to me with a smile. His eyes were warm and twinkling. "Afternoon, Glen. What can I do you for?"

"Oh, nothing. I mean, I don't need anything. I just wanted to thank you for your help yesterday. I don't think I *ever* thanked you."

"Sure you did. The look on your face when I stopped the truck was all the thanks I needed. Have you been to see the dog?"

"I was just on my way there."

"Well, I'll go with you." John put on his jacket, then called into the bay area to say he'd be back in fifteen minutes, and we walked down the block and a half to the vet's office. I said something about his not needing to come, and he just grinned and said, "Of course I'll come. If it's bad news, you'll need me there."

There was a receptionist at the desk, but when I said who I was, she called Dr. Clifton from the back room right away.

"Oh, there you are," he said as he came out. He had on plastic gloves and a white coat, and there was a lot of blood on him. I guess I looked worried, because he said, "Oh, I forgot to take this off. Two Dobermans had a fight, and one of them has a nasty gash to the head. Head wounds always bleed a lot. But they'll both live to fight again."

He peeled off the gloves and tossed them in a waste basket. "Well, come along."

John and I followed him to the back. There were a number of large cages, with dogs in several of them, including a Doberman with a bandage on its head. In the farthest cage was Scruffy, lying perfectly still on his side with bandages covering his lower body, his eyes shut.

"Is he—okay?" I gulped.

"He's alive, if that's what you mean," Dr. Clifton said. "Not to say it wasn't touch and go. There were one or two times in the night I thought I was going to lose him."

"In the night?" I asked. "You were here all night?"

"Certainly I was. You don't think I'm going to operate on him and then just leave him here, do you?"

"Oh, I thought—well, what you said—you didn't seem to care."

"If I didn't care," he said in clipped tones, "I wouldn't be a veterinarian, would I?"

I digested that. Last night, Dr. Clifton hadn't seemed interested in Scruffy. All he'd talked about was who would pay the bill and whether it was worth helping a homeless dog. But he had stayed up all night for that dog.

I remembered my conversation with Nicole about Charlie and Phil. I had told her she was judging them by the way they looked. But maybe I was too quick to judge people by how they appeared, too. Maybe a lot of people aren't the way they seem. I thought of Mr. Jackman, who has always been such a stern teacher. But his wife, Myra, is one of my mom's best friends. Maybe—

"You can pet him if you like," Dr. Clifton was saying. "He might respond." He opened the door of the cage.

I knelt down and put my hand in to touch the dog's head. His eyes opened instantly. Down past the bandages that little stump of a tail lifted once. He licked my hand.

"Smart dog," the vet said. "Knows how to get people on his side."

"Is he going to be okay?" I asked quietly, afraid of the answer.

"He has a badly broken leg. Might heal properly or might not. Shock was what nearly killed him. That and the neglect from the last two week. Pads on his feet are badly worn. He was half-starved. Likely would have been dead in another few weeks if someone hadn't taken him in. I mean without the accident."

A young blond woman in jeans brought a collie pup into the room and put him in a cage. "Oh, nice to see you again, John. How's the dog doing?"

John caught my surprised look and averted his eyes. "Pretty good, I guess," he answered her.

"You were here before?" I asked.

"Oh, I wandered in at my coffee break this morning."

"And at lunch time," the woman added with a grin. "Soon he'll be asking for a cot."

"Well, Scruffy is due for more medication now," Dr. Clifton said. "You can come by tomorrow after school again. He might be more alert then. Right now we're keeping him pretty well out so he doesn't try to move."

As John and I walked out of the office, I said, "You were here twice already?"

"Well, I've discovered that if you're going to pray for something it's good to have up-to-date information so you know exactly what to pray for."

"You were praying for Scruffy?"

"Well, of course I was. What did you think?"

"I—uh, I guess I didn't think. I mean, I'm not used to people who pray for everything."

"Oh, that's right. You said you'd only been a Christian for a short time."

"Yeah."

"Well, you'll learn."

"John," I said without thinking, "Nicole and Joyce talk about praying, and Pastor Grant prays, but I don't know anybody else who does. None of the other kids from church seem to. Not the way you do, for sure."

"Well, maybe they've never been taught how."

"Do you have to be taught?"

"Taught—or better yet shown."

"Could you show me? Because there are so many things I'm trying to pray for, but I'm not sure I'm doing it right."

"Would you like to come by tonight? We have a few people coming over to our place, mostly to pray."

"Yeah? That would be good, if you don't mind."

"Don't mind one bit."

He told me where he and Katherine were living and said to be there at seven, and then he went back to work at the garage while I went home to try to convince my parents we needed a dog.

"There's a message for you," Mom said as I walked in the kitchen. "She said she'd call back."

I got a glass of milk from the fridge and went to look at the message, expecting to see Nicole's number.

*Marta Billings called at 3:30. Will call again.*

I groaned. I've known Marta all my life, and all my life she's been a pest. But I don't remember her ever calling me before. Why would Marta call me? To apologize for the ink? Fat chance. Did I have to answer if she called back?

As if on cue, the phone rang.

Mom looked at me. Slowly, I picked up the receiver.

"Glen, I need to talk to you." It was Marta all right.

"What for," I asked warily.

Her voice came through loud and sarcastic. "Because I like talking to dweebs, of course. Why else would I want to talk to you?"

"Well, you are talking to me."

"I don't mean over the phone, you dweeb. I need to talk to you in person!"

"You'll see me at school tomorrow."

"This can't wait until tomorrow!"

"What are you up to now?"

"I'm not up to anything. I just need to talk to you. It's important."

I sighed. "When?"

"I'll meet you at Harry's in ten minutes."

Like a real dweeb, I said I would.

Then I sat for two full minutes staring at the phone. Why on earth would Marta call me? It didn't make any sense at all! She'd been a pest for as long as I can remember, and we've never been anything close to what could be called friends. Why would she need to talk to me?

I told Mom I had to go and talk to somebody and took off back downtown. If nothing else, I was getting lots of exercise these days.

Marta was alone in a booth drinking an orange pop. As soon as I stepped inside the restaurant, she looked up, pushing her long black hair back so it wasn't in the way. She had taken her coat off, and for once she was wearing something that wasn't black. The bulky red sweater really suited her. I mean it made her look sort of warm and, well, good. Except she was wearing too much lipstick and eyeshadow and all that junk some girls think they need. Marta always looks kind of—overdone. But I guess she's pretty. Well, more than pretty. Only that prettiness never seems to quite reach her eyes.

I slipped into the booth across from her and said, "You've got two minutes. What do you want?"

"Oh, Glen, I'm so glad you came. I'm in trouble and I need your help."

"What kind of help?" I didn't believe her for one minute.

"It's not something I want to talk about. I mean, not just like that. I need to explain."

"So explain already."

"You're not exactly helping. You act as if I were going to bite or something."

"Knowing you, that's entirely possible. What do you want?"

"It's about Charlie."

I rolled my eyes. Who else would it be about? Everywhere I went, it was Charlie!

"Why don't you get a drink? It'll take a couple of minutes for me to tell it all."

"I'm not thirsty." That wasn't true, but I didn't want her to think I was staying a second longer than I absolutely had to.

"You're making me nervous. I can't talk when I'm nervous."

I gave up. "Fine, I'll get a drink, take my coat off, and relax. Then you've got ten minutes to tell me your problem or I'm out of here."

"It's about Charlie," she repeated when I was back.

"You already told me that. Go on."

"You know we went out a lot last fall?"

"Sure, I know that."

"Well, I really like him, Glen."

"Sure, you do." I studied my root beer.

"No, I mean I *really* like him. Even though I found out he was only using me to make Nicole jealous, I still like him."

"So what's the point?"

"I want to get him back. I mean, I want him to like me. To forget about Nicole."

"So talk to Charlie, not me." I took a long drink.

"I can't go up to him and say, 'Forget about Nicole and date me.' But what about if you help me? I know he still thinks he wants Nicole, but that's mostly because she's playing hard-to-get. I'm sure once he had her he'd get tired of her really fast. I mean, what do they have in common? Nothing, really."

I could have thought of a few things, but I wasn't going to discuss them with Marta. "So what exactly do you want me to do?" I asked. "Not that I plan to do it."

"It's easy. Just let Nicole date Charlie a couple of times. He'll stop being interested in her, and then I'll get him back." She batted her eyelashes and bit her lip.

"Sorry," I said easily. "I couldn't get Nicole to date him even if I wanted to. You'd do better to talk to her."

"I couldn't talk to her."

"Why not?"

"She doesn't like me."

"Nicole likes everybody."

Marta gave me a long searching look from under those artificial lashes. "She sure has you fooled."

I stood up. "Is that all you wanted?"

"There must be *something* that you could do to help me! Glen, I'm desperate!"

I was almost laughing now. "Cut out the dramatics, Marta! I don't buy it."

"Maybe you'll buy this," she said quietly, jumping up and stepping into my path. She put her arms around me and kissed me, right in the middle of Harry's! Then she said, out loud for everyone to hear, "Oh, Glen, you're terrific! I'll be waiting tonight!"

By the time I had snapped out of shock, she was gone and I was standing there looking like a complete fool.

When I got home, Mom and Dad were both there. I wanted to tell them what had happened and get some sympathy, but I was afraid they'd laugh. Anybody would. But it was impossible to figure out what Marta was up to. She'd done enough crazy things in the past for this to be just one more. Yet I couldn't help thinking there was something behind it. But what?

Fortunately for my overworked brain, I had little time to wonder about Marta. We had dinner, and sat around the table talking about Mom's new job and about Phil. They knew I'd been to see him, but I couldn't exactly tell them what had happened, so I just said he seemed to be pretty well his usual self, except of course that he couldn't move.

I waited till they had talked themselves out and then I said, "You know, it's been kind of lonely around here lately."

They both stared at me.

"Well, you know, I'm the only one at home."

"Glen," Dad said dryly, "you've been the only one at home for several years."

"Well, I haven't been as busy out of the house as I used to be."

"What do you want, Glen?" Dad asked in his no-nonsense kind of voice.

"A dog," I replied.

"Oh, Glen," Mom said in her "you know we can't" voice.

"Not just *any* dog," I explained hastily. I told about finding Scruffy and how he'd been hit by a car and all—I didn't say a word about Charlie—and how Dr. Clifton had operated and thought he might be okay, and how he'd licked my hand, and how he'd already been abandoned once and I couldn't just abandon him, too.

I must have done a reasonably good job because Mom had tears in her eyes when I finished.

Dad cleared his throat. "Glen, you've made a good case, but you're dealing with emotional issues. Somebody will have to pay the vet's fee and get a leash and a collar and all the other things a dog needs. Then there's the day-to-day feeding and walking and brushing and other kinds of care. Not only that, but with your mother's new job, the dog would be left alone for a good part of the day. And next year, when you're away at college, what would we do?"

"Yeah, I guess I never thought about next year," I said, hanging my head. That was my problem—I didn't think.

But I did realize this was no time to argue about whether or not I was actually going to college next year.

"Your dad and I will discuss it later, Glen. Maybe we can think of another family that would take him."

I went to my room and lay down on the bed. Nothing was working out.

Suddenly I remembered John and his invitation. I was already late.

# 9

I ran to the kitchen and asked if I could borrow the car.

"Sorry, Glen, I have to go out. Can I drop you off?"

"Yeah, sure." I didn't know how to explain to Dad about John, but it turned out I didn't need to. When I gave the address, and mentioned that I'd met John and Katherine at the Grants' and that he was working in Winter's Garage, Dad said, "Oh, yes. He stopped by to say hello today just before I left the bank. Said he'd invited you over and wanted me to know who he was. Seemed like a nice young man."

"Yeah," I said. I felt kind of dazed again. "He is. So's his wife. She's having a baby soon."

"Oh? Let your mother know so she can crochet something for you to give the baby."

He dropped me off, no problem, and I found the apartment easily. Truth is, there are very few apartment blocks in Wallace, and the ones we have are small, so there are only about eight apartments in each.

Katherine answered the door. There were three other people in the living room. Besides Katherine and John, I mean. One was a thin elderly man who lived in the apartment block. Katherine introduced him as Mr. Smithers. The other two were a guy named Pete Ferahowsky and his wife. Pete was in school with my sister Janice, so he's about twenty-three or four. I think his wife is younger. Pete is big, with long brown hair and tattoos and a motorcycle. He does odd jobs, moving people and digging up stumps and all sorts of things. His wife, Colleen, who is tiny and blonde, works in the hotel as a maid. I knew who they were but I've never really talked to them. It never would have occurred to me that either of them would have any interest in praying. But if John said so....

Katherine gave me a can of root beer, and then John asked us all to tell where we lived when we were nine, and what kind of car our family had, and when God first became real to us.

Pete and Colleen and I had lived in Wallace all our lives, but it turned out Mr. Smithers had been born and raised in London, England, and hadn't come to America until after the Second World War. Katherine had lived in Chicago until she was eleven, and John was from a small town in California.

Mr. Smithers was the only one whose parents hadn't owned a car. His family had walked or taken a trolley.

As for when we first became aware of God, Mr. Smithers said for him it was in the war when he was on an island in the Pacific, and he got wounded. He thought he'd die, and he told God if he made it out alive, he would believe there was a God.

Pete said he'd always known there was a God, but he only got to know him last week when John and he had coffee and John introduced him to Jesus.

Colleen shyly said she'd always thought there was a God, and she'd like to know him better. She glanced sideways at Pete and said, "Especially now that Pete don't mind."

Katherine and John said they'd become aware of God two years ago when their first baby was born with heart problems and died. They had been so upset they had gone to a neighbor who they knew had a strong faith, and he had helped them give their lives to God.

After that, we sang a couple of songs out of a small book John gave out, and then we spent some time talking about our lives and praying for each other.

I told them a little bit about Phil and how I'd messed up, and how I didn't know much about girls and wasn't doing so great with Nicole, and how I had no idea what to do about Charlie. I also told about the dog and about Marta, and how my life was kind of upside down.

When I finished, they prayed for me, most of them kind of shy and stumbling; but all of them prayed, even old Mr. Smithers. I prayed for them, too, after they had told us their problems. It was really neat.

After that, Pete and Colleen and Mr. Smithers left right away. I stayed a few minutes talking about Scruffy and my parents' reaction. John told me not to worry; that it would likely be a while before the dog would be well enough to go anywhere. Anything could happen.

I agreed.

He offered me a ride home, but I said I'd rather walk.

"Do you think you'd like to come back next week?"

I said, "Yeah," without even thinking. I told him that this was my idea of what Christians should do when they got together. This was what I'd been wanting when I was sitting in the youth group meeting last Sunday feeling frustrated. Sure, I needed to learn more about the Bible and how to live as a Christian, but I also needed to know that people cared about me and the problems I was having. It felt really good praying for them, too.

"We'll be meeting at Pete and Colleen's," Katherine said, "so we'll pick you up if you like."

Then I walked home. Man, so much had happened to me in the last few days that my head was spinning. Which reminded me—after all the work Nicole had had me doing the first while back after Christmas, the last few days I hadn't done anything.

How I was supposed to find the energy to think about schoolwork was more than I knew.

I was almost at Charlie's house when I realized his car was in the driveway and someone was sitting in it. With everything else going on, I'd forgotten all about Charlie.

A car door slammed, and sure enough, Charlie stood up.

We stared at each other with the street between us.

"You ready to give up Nicole yet?" he shouted.

"You idiot," I said half-heartedly.

"You can't keep her, you know."

Remembering something Nicole had said, I called out, "Did nobody ever tell you that you can't have everything you want?"

"Says who?"

"Says me."

"What do you know about girls?"

"Enough to know they aren't all crazy about you."

"Yeah? There isn't a single girl in this town who isn't crazy about me."

"You really think so? What if I told them how you nearly killed a dog? Do you think they'd like you if they found out you just drove away and left it to die?"

"I never did!"

"Yes, you did! You hit a dog on the road yesterday. It's at the vet's right now, no thanks to you! The only person you ever think about is yourself! If you keep on like that, before long you won't have *any* friends!" I turned and walked quickly into my house.

He shouted something else, but I didn't listen.

"Marta called again," Mom told me when I got inside. "I didn't know you and she were—I mean, I thought you were going with Nicole."

"Marta has several screws loose in her brain."

"Perhaps the fact that you've been dating Nicole makes other girls notice you more."

I gave a noncommittal, "Maybe." The only problem was that Marta wasn't like other girls. She wasn't like anything human.

"You're growing up," Mom said.

I looked at her, wondering what she was thinking.

"Oh, I don't mind, you know," she said. "It's just that, well, you are my youngest—and that makes you sort of special."

I busied myself getting a glass of milk and some of the freshly made cookies. I'm not good at mushy. Fortunately, Mom seldom gets mushy.

"But one of these days my baby will be married with a family of his own. And that will be great!" she said.

"I'm not in a big rush, you know, Mom."

"I know. At least, I hope you aren't. Not that Nicole isn't a nice girl. She is, and I like her very much. But it's all been rather sudden, and I hope you won't get carried away."

"I won't."

She smiled. "Good."

"Mom—" I said after a few minutes of silence "—how did you know Dad was the right one?"

"Well, he wasn't the first boy I dated, but I guess I wasn't that much older than you when I decided he was the one. We just sort of fit. Things I thought were funny, he thought were funny, too. Our minds seemed to mesh."

"That's weird."

"But it worked."

"Yeah."

"There's no rush, Glen. The right person will never insist that you hurry into anything."

"Yeah? Nicole isn't like that. She's—well, she's sensitive, I guess."

"That's good."

Mom was cleaning up the kitchen. She looked over at me every now and then, and I could tell she wanted to say something. Finally, she coughed.

"Yeah, Mom?" I asked.

"Well, I was just wondering. It's been several months since you started going to church. Do you—enjoy going, Glen?"

"Yeah, I guess." My parents knew nothing about my decision to ask Jesus to take over my life, and I really didn't know how to tell them. One of these days, I would have to say something.

But not now. I looked at the clock and realized I still had homework to do. "Yeah, it's okay," I said. I got out of there in a hurry.

The next day went fine until after classes when I met Nicole at her locker. She looked upset, and I had a sinking feeling in my stomach that it was because of something I'd done.

"Going to Harry's?" I asked.

"No." That was all she said. Just, "No."

"Is anything wrong?"

"No."

"Nicole, I know something is wrong. What is it?"

"Nothing is wrong. It's not like you have to tell me everything you do. Your life is your own."

Now I knew for sure it had something to do with me. "Nicole, if I've done something, tell me. I don't know."

"It's okay, Glen," she said evenly. "I'm not angry with you. I'm angry with myself for being upset. I shouldn't be."

"What are you upset about?" I asked again.

"You have a right to go out with anyone you want."

"What are you talking about?" I shouted in exasperation, then realized other kids were standing around listening to us. I lowered my voice. "Why don't I walk you home and we can talk about this."

"No, thanks. I'm walking home with—with Paul."

She turned away and ran to catch up with her brother, who had just gone by with a couple of his friends. I stood watching her and shaking my head. What else could possibly go wrong?

I thought about following her, but I knew my first priority was to go and talk to Phil again. I didn't want to, but after messing up so badly yesterday, I had to say something.

He was alone, and upside down again. At first I thought he was sleeping. I was about to tiptoe back out, but as I reached the door he said, "What do *you* want?" in a low voice.

"I—uh—I just came by to see how you are. And to—to apologize for yesterday. I'm sorry I kind of preached at you."

"It doesn't matter." His voice was flat and listless, nothing like normal.

I went closer and sat on a chair next to him. "You not feeling very good? Does it hurt much?"

He gave a sort of half-laugh. "If it hurt, I'd feel a lot better. Pain I can take. The problem is that it doesn't hurt. I can't feel a thing."

Words failed me.

"And this place is the pits!" he said. "I'm going crazy in here!"

"It must be rough," I sympathized.

"Rough!" He snorted in disgust.

"When will they let you go home?"

"They're talking about sending me to some other place. They say they aren't equipped to do rehab here. I'm healing okay, and soon I'll need to go someplace where I can learn how to live with this—this—!" He swore.

I tried to change the subject. "How's the food?"

"Lousy. And these old ladies keep coming in to wash me and take my temperature and change the bed and tell me not to be impatient. And they always laugh! Like it's some big joke that I'm lying here helpless having all these old women working me over."

"I guess they're trying to cheer you up," I said tentatively.

"Well, they aren't." He gritted his teeth and wrinkled his brow. "It's maddening!"

"I wish—well, I wish there were something I could do."

"There doesn't seem to be anything anybody can do." He sounded hopeless. Not at all like Phil.

I had no idea what to say to cheer him up. Then it occurred to me that he couldn't see me all that well in his mirror, so I lay down on the floor beside his bed. "Do you want me to read to you or something?"

"Don't get carried away."

"I'm not. I just—well, I don't know what to do!"

"As long as you don't start telling me about God again."

"Don't worry. I won't."

We stared at each other.

Then he said, softly, "Why don't you tell me about school. What's happening?"

I folded my arms up behind my head to make a pillow and told him about Marta's phone call and the weird scene at Harry's, and I guess I really drew it out. He seemed to think it was pretty funny. We talked about Marta and how she's such a loony, and then I told him everything I could remember about the teachers and classes and every dumb thing I could recall doing lately.

Only I didn't tell him about Charlie and the dog and all that.

And I stayed clear of anything that even remotely touched on God or the church.

By the time the nurse came in and kicked me out, he seemed a little happier. As I went to the door, he said, "Say hello to the teachers for me. That's the only good part of this. At least I get to miss school."

"Should I come back tomorrow?"

"That'd be great. If you have time."

"I've got lots of time."

"What about Nicole? You never mentioned her."

"Oh, she's okay."

"You still going with her? Charlie hasn't got her yet?"

I neglected to mention that she seemed to be mad at me at the moment and just said, "Yep. I'm still going with her. Charlie's still in the cold."

"Weird."

"Yeah, I know. Well, I'll see you tomorrow."

"Okay."

I trudged over to the vet's, feeling good that Phil seemed to want my company, but bad that he couldn't do anything but lie there. I prayed they could send him to some other doctor who would be able to find something they had missed and make him better.

Dr. Clifton was talking to the receptionist as I went in, and he motioned for me to go on into the back room. Scruffy was still lying there, but his eyes were open. As soon as he saw me, his ears seemed to prick up and his crazy little tail started thumping.

I opened the door of his cage and put my hand in to rub his head. He licked my hand.

"Looking pretty good, isn't he," Dr. Clifton said from behind me. "Look at those clear eyes. That's one smart dog."

"How's his leg?"

"The trick is going to be getting him to let it heal. Dogs are funny. Some of them will worry an injury so much it can't heal. Others seem to know it takes time and will just rest and let it take its course."

I looked at Scruffy, lying there licking my hand. From what I had seen, he was smart enough to know his leg needed time.

"He should be ready to go home with you in a few days, but you'll have to have a kennel to keep him in. Otherwise, he'll be more apt to try to walk around. You'll have to keep a close eye on him, carry the kennel into your room at night, and so forth."

Home? A few days? What was he saying? But my parents had said no! What on earth was I going to do?

I don't know what I said. "Okay," I think. But I knew I couldn't just show up at home with the dog.

I left shortly after that. It was nearly five-thirty. I knew Dad would be leaving the bank about now. But for some reason, my steps headed towards Winter's Garage.

John was outside, doing something to the engine of the tow truck.

"Dog's looking pretty good," he said when he saw me.

"Yeah," I said. I guess I sounded the way I felt, because he gave me a funny look.

"You don't seem as happy as I thought you would."

"He's nearly ready for me to take him home."

"Really? That was quick! God's sure at work."

"Well, I wish God would do something about changing my parents' minds."

"Yes, you've definitely got a problem there. Maybe if they saw the dog?" he suggested.

"Maybe. I'll try to get them to come down tomorrow."

"How's Phil?"

I told him about my visit to the hospital, and then he said, right there on the street, "Well, we really need to pray." And he did. Just said, "Lord, here are some concerns we have..." and started praying about Scruffy and Mom and Dad and Phil, not caring who came by or heard.

Afterwards, I thanked him and headed home. In his own way, John was just as disconcerting as Marta.

After dinner, I decided I'd better call Nicole. Paul answered the phone and told me she was busy. I asked if he'd get her to call back. He didn't promise.

When nothing had happened by eight-thirty, I called again. Again, Paul answered and said she was busy. That's all. Just "busy."

I finally gave up and turned on the TV.

Dad wasn't back from his meeting and Mom had gone over to a neighbor's, so I turned it really loud to keep me from thinking.

The red Mercedes did a brake-squealing turn in the middle of the freeway. Tires shrieked, horns blared, but the driver ignored them as he brought his car under control and found some driving room. His speedometer shot up. Ahead of him, the truck he was following careened drunkenly as it weaved in and out of traffic. Sooner or later, somebody would make a mistake and the sirens of ambulances would smother out the memory of the squealing tires—

The phone rang. I ignored it, but it rang again. "Mom!" I yelled. I remembered it might be Nicole and reached for the remote to turn down the volume.

"Nicole?" My voice sounded anxious even to my ears.

"Glen?" It wasn't her voice.

"Yeah?"

"It's me. Marta."

"Marta?" I probably sounded disgusted. That's sure how I felt.

"Yes. Marta!" she said with emphasis. "What's going on there? Sounds like somebody's leaning on a car horn."

"Just the TV."

"Do you really need it that loud?"

"I already turned it down."

"You did, huh? Well, anyway, I need to talk."

"Yeah, right," I said.

"No, I *really* need to talk. There's something you should know."

"Just like yesterday. How dumb do you think I am?"

"Glen, you're a dope." She sounded like she was crying. "This *is* about yesterday."

"Forget it." I hung up on her. I might be an idiot, but I wasn't enough of one to get any more involved with her than I already was.

The phone rang again and I ignored it.

The Mercedes had caught up to the truck and the two vehicles were snaking through heavy traffic at high speed. Muted horns vied with the phone for my attention.

On the fifth ring, Mom walked into the house and hurried to pick up the phone. "Glen, it's for you," she called. "Why didn't you answer?"

I picked up the receiver. "Marta, I told you I can't meet you tonight!"

There was a small gasp and a click. The line went dead.

A feeling of horror swept over me. No. It couldn't have been!

On the TV screen, the Mercedes was neck and neck with the cab of the truck. The truck driver, a big bearded guy, was laughing as he nudged the small car, trying to send it over a steep cliff.

I quickly dialed Nicole's number and once more got Paul. "I really don't think she wants to talk to you," he said.

"Did she just try to call me?" I asked, my heart sinking rapidly into my feet.

"I think so. But she doesn't want to talk now. Look, could you bother her at school tomorrow? I've got a lot of homework to do."

I hung up and lay back on the couch. Why was I such an idiot? Why?

On the screen, the driver of the Mercedes picked up a revolver and neatly wiped the smile off the truck driver's face. The truck zigzagged across the road, missing the Mercedes by inches, and plunged over the edge of the cliff.

At the same time, my thoughts plunged into total despair.

At school the next day, Nicole simply ignored me. The one time I got close enough to talk to her, she just said, "I don't want to talk about it," and walked away. The only cheerful thing was that Joyce gave me a kind of smile, like maybe she understood how I felt.

We had a math test, but my mind was incapable of concentrating. Who cared about math when all these other more important things were happening?

After school, Brett and Mac talked me into going to Harry's with them. They said they'd go with me to visit Phil after we'd had a Coke. Not really caring what I did, I agreed.

But nothing was simple these days. Not even a drink at Harry's.

We hadn't been there more than a couple of minutes when Marta and her friend Dianne walked in. I drank my milkshake and ignored them, but Marta walked over and sat down next to me.

"So, how's the boy?" she said.

Marta sounded her normal self. She usually tries to make out like she's about ten years older than me and I'm a stupid moron.

"I'm fine," I said.

"Thanks for being so willing to talk last night."

"You're welcome," I said as I looked into her eyes and saw something there. Something hard.

She was still talking. "You know I used to think Charlie was terrific, but you're so much more interesting than Charlie."

I choked on my drink. Looking across the booth, I saw Brett and Mac staring at me like they'd never seen me before.

"She's nutty," I explained.

"Nutty about you," she purred. That's the only word for how she sounded. Like a cat.

Dianne came over with two Cokes, a chocolate bar, and a bag of chips. She giggled as she squeezed in beside Marta, pushing Marta against me, and me against the wall. Marta is a pain, but at least she's reasonably good-looking. Dianne always looks like she got dressed in the dark in a hurry and she acts like she has no brains whatsoever.

Dianne gave Marta a Coke and a chocolate bar, and began to open her own bag of chips. Would you believe she couldn't do it? I mean, a four-year-old can handle a bag of chips, but not Dianne. After watching her for a minute, I finally reached over, grabbed it from her, and tore it open. All she did was giggle.

Marta just sipped her drink and observed. She's always done that. As though life goes on merely so she can watch and make comments on how dumb everybody else is. She likely allows Dianne to hang around just because she likes to watch her do dumb things.

I quickly finished my milkshake, and was about to ask them both to move when Marta said, "So, are you and Charlie still friends?"

"Sure," I said. I wasn't about to discuss my life with Marta.

She stated calmly. "He's a—" She used a word I didn't think girls used.

"Really? You used to like him well enough," I retorted. "Like two days ago when you were asking me to help you get him back."

"Not really." She smiled up at me under those long artificial lashes.

"That's what you told me."

"That was just an excuse to see you. You're the one I'm interested in." And as if to prove it, she put her hand on my knee and squeezed.

# 10

I reached down and pulled her hand up. She immediately reached for my knee again, and this time I grabbed her hand and held it. She snuggled her head against my shoulder. I felt trapped—shoved against the wall on a bench seat, with the high chair back behind, the table in front, and a five-foot-five cobra wedged in beside me.

"You're so sweet," she said, sounding as though she meant it.

"Let me out of here." I started to push her and Dianne out of my way. Dianne giggled and Marta said something stupid, like, "Oh, Glen, sweetie, you're so impatient!"

At which point Charlie walked in.

I didn't see who Charlie was with, but they sat down in the booth right behind us. I didn't know if he'd seen us or not.

In as determined a voice as I could manage, but not loud enough for anyone else (like Charlie) to hear, I said, "Let me out, Marta. Or I'm going to start yelling for help.

She smiled at me.

Brett and Mac were sitting across from us with their mouths open.

I whispered loudly at them, "Do something you idiots! Get me out of here."

I was wondering if I could slide under the table when out of the corner of my eye I saw Marta pick up her glass, which was still half-full, and get up on her knees in the booth so she could see behind. I wasn't fast enough to guess what she had in mind, so I could only watch as she poured her drink, ice cubes and all, on Charlie's head.

Of course, I didn't actually see it land on Charlie's head. But I saw him jump up with his head dripping and a couple of ice cubes caught in his collar, and I heard what he said to Marta, which I won't repeat because it was the kind of language you wouldn't use if you thought Jesus was around. Of course, Charlie wasn't thinking about Jesus being around.

Marta had collapsed onto the seat and was sort of hiding behind Dianne. Both of them were giggling their heads off. Well, Dianne sure was. Marta was laughing, but it wasn't a nice laugh.

Then Charlie was in front of our booth, yelling at Marta. When he saw me, he stopped in mid-shout and a strange light came into his eyes. "Well, Glen, I suppose this was your idea?" He was purring, just like Marta had been earlier.

I shook my head.

"I'll bet."

"Honest, it wasn't."

Marta and Dianne kept giggling. I wondered why these things keep happening to me. And what I could say to calm Charlie down.

"I'll get both of you for this," Charlie said softly. "And don't think I won't." Then he went to the wash room to get cleaned off.

I told Marta she was crazy, and with some help from Brett and Mac managed to get both girls out of the booth. Dianne was still giggling. I grabbed Marta's hand and pulled her to the door. "Get going," I said, "before Harry finds out what you did."

She gave me a funny look.

"Go on," I said. "No doubt he deserved it, but it was a stupid thing to do. But then, you do a lot of stupid things, don't you?"

I tossed some money at Harry, who was busy behind the counter waiting on a couple of young boys who couldn't decide what they wanted, and pushed both girls outside.

"Have you got your car?" I asked Marta. She often drives her dad's car.

She nodded.

"Then be sensible for once and go home," I advised her.

"You're a doll," she said, and before I could stop her she leaned forward and kissed me again.

Without even looking for Brett and Mac, I turned and ran.

I went to the hospital but Phil wasn't in his room and the nurse at the desk mumbled something about more tests, so I went to the vet's and spent half an hour with Scruffy. As he had the day before, he seemed to know who I was and he thumped his tail and licked me like crazy. I still had no idea what to do with him, and with so much other stuff happening, I hadn't had much time to concentrate on finding a solution.

I was halfway home when I realized I had to go and talk to Nicole. But when I got to her house, her youngest sister told me she was spending the night at Joyce's so they could work on some sewing project.

I went home and tried to concentrate on homework. I knew Nicole wouldn't think much of me if I failed all my classes.

I mentioned the dog again at dinner. In fact, I tried to pour it on, hoping I would touch Mom's sympathetic side. I described his little thumping tail, and how he licked my hand, and everything I could think of. I think Mom was weakening a little, but Dad just said he'd try to think of a family that would want him. He asked, "Won't the veterinarian costs be high, Glen?" Banker's always think of financial matters sooner or later. Generally sooner.

"Yeah, I guess so."

"Who is paying for them?"

I gulped. "I am."

"You are?" He didn't sound very pleased.

"I have money in the bank."

"I thought that money was going toward college."

All the frustration I'd been feeling over the last week kind of boiled over. I stood up and leaned toward him. "Yeah, that's what *you* thought. Because *you* keep talking about me going to college. But *I* never said I was going. I don't even know what I want to do. Anyway, it's *my* money. I earned it, and I'll spend it the way I want! I'm going to spend all of it on Scruffy if I have to. And I know that's a stupid name for a dog!"

I ran to my room, slammed the door, and threw myself on the bed. Now I felt like a complete idiot. Especially when I realized there were tears in my eyes. Charlie wouldn't cry no matter what. Phil probably hadn't even cried over his injury. But stupid Glen cried over a dopey little dog!

Mom and Dad wisely left me alone. About eleven, I went out and found them sitting in the living room, watching the news and talking. I told them I was sorry, and they said they understood. They said they knew I was upset because of what had happened to Phil, and that it was okay. They even said if I wanted the dog that much, I could have it here until we found a better place.

That should have made me feel better, but it didn't. All I could think of was that David wouldn't have tried to get his way by having a tantrum.

The next morning was Saturday. I knew I couldn't take another day of getting no answer at Nicole's, so at nine o'clock I asked Dad if I could borrow the car and I drove out to the Burgess's farm. Their collie started barking as soon as I pulled into the yard, and Joyce opened the back door.

After yelling at the dog to be quiet, she called out, "We're having waffles, Glen. Come on in."

"Thanks, but I've had breakfast. I need to talk to Nicole for a minute. I can wait outside till she's finished eating."

"Don't be silly. Come in."

I took off my shoes, but not my jacket.

Nicole was sitting at the table, her plate nearly empty.

"I have to talk to you," I said. She looked up at me with those big green eyes, and the way she looked reminded me of the way Scruffy had looked at me. I immediately forgot the words I had planned to say, and I just stood there stammering, "I—I—you—we—"

It might have gone on for ever, but she stood up and said, "I'll get my jacket and come out."

So we went outside and walked slowly along the road to the mailbox.

"Nicole," I finally said.

"What?" She didn't look at me.

"You have to let me explain. I know what you think, but it isn't true."

She looked straight at me, her eyes questioning. "What isn't true?"

"I figured out what you were saying the other day. About my being able to be with anyone I wanted. You think I was with Marta on Wednesday, don't you? Well, I wasn't. At least, I was, but not really. I didn't do anything!"

"You have every right to be with anybody you want and to do anything you want."

"But the only girl I want to be with is you."

"I don't care that you were with Marta, Glen. What I do mind is your lying to me about it. You can go out with her if you want, but I expect you to tell me you're dating her and not do it behind my back. I don't want to date somebody who isn't honest."

"But I wasn't, really. No matter what you heard—"

"Glen, I saw you with my own eyes yesterday."

"You did?"

"Yes!"

I opened my mouth to explain what had happened, but she said, "Don't try to explain. I don't want you to have to tell any more lies."

"I don't tell lies."

She looked at me.

"Well, not about important things."

"As I said the other day, I guess I'm not very important to you."

"Nicole, Marta called me Wednesday and asked me to meet her at Harry's. She said she had to talk to me. I have no idea what she wanted or why she kissed me. Thursday she called again, wanting to meet me again. I hung up on her. When you called, I thought it was her calling back."

"And yesterday? At Harry's? When you were with her in the booth and then left with her and kissed her in the middle of the street?"

"How do you know all that? Did Charlie tell you?"

"Charlie didn't need to tell me. I was there. I saw you myself. You didn't look all that upset to be with Marta when I saw you."

"You were there?"

"Charlie offered to give me a ride to Joyce's. We stopped at Harry's on the way. You were there with Marta."

I felt angry now. What right had she to be mad at me over Marta when she'd been with Charlie? "I hope you and Charlie had a nice time together," I said sarcastically.

"You were the one who told me I should talk to him," she replied.

What could I say to that? She was right.

She went on. "And you don't seem to have been too concerned about me these last few days. I've barely seen you since Sunday."

"That's because—well, so much has been happening."

"You seem to have time for Marta."

Of all the stupid things I could have said, I remembered what Marta had said about Nicole on Wednesday. "Marta says you don't like her."

"Did the two of you have a nice time discussing me?" she asked. Tears came to her eyes and she turned away.

"Nicole—"

She turned back toward me, and now she was really angry. "Aren't you going to tell me about the good time you had at the movie Saturday night? Or did you think that because you drove to Stanton I wouldn't hear about it? I can't believe I could be such a fool as to think you were different from other guys!" She started running toward the house, crying for real. I began to follow, but there wasn't much point. Looked like I'd really blown it.

Mom was in the kitchen when I got home two hours later, after driving halfway across the county and back. I guess I was okay by then. At least Mom didn't seem to notice anything.

"While you were gone, I walked over to the animal hospital, Glen. I saw the dog, and I told Dr. Clifton we'd get him Tuesday after school. We'll have to stop at the hardware first and pick up a few things. He seemed like a nice dog. Dr. Clifton said he's very intelligent, and very good-natured. He showed me how to take care of the leg."

"Oh."

She looked more closely at me. "You don't sound very thrilled."

"I'm sorry. It's just—Mom, is growing up always this hard?"

She sat on one of the kitchen chairs. "Well, Glen, it was different for each of your brother and sisters, but yes, for several growing up was very hard. I can still remember how upset

Carrie was when she didn't get invited to her senior prom. She said she knew no man would ever be interested in her. And when Jordan failed to get into the college he wanted, he thought that was the end of the world. But it turned out to be the best thing for him."

"What about when they were dating and stuff. Did they ever—was if sometimes frustrating?"

"I guess you don't remember when Janice and Ron had that fight a month before their wedding and they almost called the whole thing off. Relationships are often difficult."

"Did any of them have a friend who got paralyzed?"

"No, but do you remember Bud Kirchen, Janice's friend?"

I vaguely remembered someone named Bud.

"He was killed in a car accident in grade eleven. He and Janice had been dating. That was pretty hard for her."

"Yeah," I agreed, thinking how I would feel if Nicole were killed.

"These things happen, Glen. All the time. Sometimes they happen to people we know. Like Frank Jackman. He's dying and there's nothing his family and friends can do."

"Mom?"

"Yes, Glen?"

"Do you believe there's a God?"

"Yes, I guess I do."

"Do you think he cares about what happens?"

"I guess. I'm not sure he can do a lot, though."

"What do you mean?"

"Well, things happen. I don't know if he can control them or not."

"You mean he's there but not really in control?"

"I'm not sure. I guess I haven't really thought about it much."

"Do you think there's a heaven?"

"Yes, I think so."

"How do you get there?"

She shrugged. "Well, I guess by doing your best to live right. Not breaking the law."

"Do you think most people go to heaven when they die?"

"Yes, I guess so. I don't think we can really know for sure."

"Do you ever pray?"

"Sometimes." She looked at me intently. "You sure have a lot of heavy questions today."

"Yeah, I guess." I stood up. "Thanks for going to the vet's, Mom. I guess we'll see what happens." I went to my room to do some homework.

Instead, I pulled out my Bible. It had been several days since I'd looked at it. I turned to the book called First Samuel and read some more about David. I even found a place where he took another man's wife and then had the man killed. Some great guy! I don't think you could exactly say he lived right. Murder is definitely against the law.

The only thing was, as soon as this guy Nathan called David out on what he'd done, he immediately confessed to God. I guess that's what makes the difference. We may get off track and do something wrong, but when we realize it was wrong, we have to admit that and not lie about it or make excuses. And we have to accept the consequences and try not to make the same mistake again.

In the afternoon, I followed what was getting to be a routine of going to visit Phil and then Scruffy. Phil was right side up for a change.

"This stinks," he said when I went in. There was a magazine lying near him on the bed and he picked it up and threw it on the floor.

"Yeah." I couldn't imagine what he felt like, but I knew it must be awful. Especially for someone who was normally as active as he was.

He changed the subject. "So how are things going?"

I told him about yesterday at Harry's, and about Nicole's being mad at me because of Marta. And how she'd let Charlie drive her to Joyce's. "I guess he's finally won," I said.

He actually laughed. "Now you know what it's like. You used to think I was crazy because Lisa was always getting annoyed with me."

"I didn't think Nicole was like that."

"She's female, isn't she?"

"Yeah, but she's a Christian, Phil. I thought she was different because of that."

"Don't get off on that God-stuff again," he warned.

"No, I'm not. But I really did think she was different because of that." I turned to face him. "Phil, am I different? Since I became a Christian, I mean? Don't I seem to be different?"

"You're a lot less fun, if that's what you mean. But that might be because of Nicole."

"Come on Phil."

"Well, you worry a lot more."

Not exactly what I had hoped to hear. "I'm really blowing everything."

"Come on, Glen, you can't solve everybody's problems."

"I can't even solve my own."

"Like I can?" he asked bitterly.

Neither of us said anything for a few minutes. Then he spoke. "Glen, I'm going to make this easy for you." He looked away from me. "When this is all settled over Charlie and Nicole, if you decide you want to be Charlie's friend again, I'll understand. After all, he can walk around."

I just looked at him.

"I mean it, Glen. You can be Charlie's friend. I don't care."

"I never said I wanted to be his friend. Why should I?"

"Why shouldn't you? Everybody likes him. He's got the car and the girls and everything. He always comes out on top. So it's okay."

"Well, if I ever decide I want to be friends with him, I'll let you know. But don't hold your breath."

"There's just one thing." His voice was low and I could hear the tension in it. "I hate him, Glen. I know he saved my life, but I hate him. So when you and he become friends again, just don't come back here. That's all."

"Phil, I—"

"Get out, Glen."

"But—"

"I said get out. I don't want you coming here to visit me because you feel sorry for me. I rolled the car and I'll pay for it. It's not your problem. You go live your life and forget about me." He was still talking low and I could hear pain in every word. "I've thought it over. Anyway, I won't be here much longer. I have to go to the city to learn how to live as a—a paraplegic," he spat out the word. "So go on. You have your own life to live."

"Phil, I—"

"Get lost, Glen. It's not your fault and I don't want you coming here any more. You just bug me."

He pushed a button and a nurse appeared at the door a moment later. He asked her to turn the bed and she kicked me out.

The last thing I saw was Phil lying there, his face pale and unhappy.

I wandered over to the vet's to see Scruffy. At least he was glad to have me around.

Then I stopped by the garage. John was alone, putting new snow tires on somebody's car. When he saw me, he came right over, wiping his hands on a towel.

"How's it going, Glen?" he said heartily.

I brought him up to date on Phil and Nicole. "I sure wish I knew what to do," I said.

"Well, Glen, there are times when you have to realize there isn't anything you can do."

I looked at him.

"Sometimes it isn't your problem. Sometimes it's the other person who has to do the doing."

I guess my face looked as dumb as I felt.

"Take David, for instance. You were telling me you've been reading about him. Have you got to the part where he sinned with Bathsheba and then had her husband killed?"

I nodded.

"Well, the prophet Nathan came and told David that he'd done wrong. Now, it was Nathan's responsibility to confront David. God had given him that to do. If he had been afraid to do it, that would have been a problem between him and God. Do you follow?"

I nodded again.

"Well, Nathan did it. I don't for one minute think it was an easy thing to go before that powerful and very popular king and say, in essence, 'You've just messed up your life and your relationship with God!' But he did.

"Now, whose responsibility was it to see that David felt sorry for what he'd done? Was it Nathan's?"

I shook my head. "No, it was David's."

"Right! Now, you've told Phil he needs God. Whose responsibility is it to take the next step?"

"Phil's," I said, finally understanding what John was getting at.

"Exactly. Whose responsibility is it to settle this with Nicole?"

"Mine to explain it, but hers to listen and to make sure she has all the facts?"

"Hey, you're a fast learner. You can't live another person's life for them. Sometimes we might like to try, but we can't. We can pray, and do what God gives us to do, but we can't make a decision for anyone else."

I nodded. I felt a lot better, as though a weight had been lifted from my shoulders.

"By the way, Glen. There's an interesting sidebar to the story of David and Nathan. Often we don't like people who point out our faults. But can you guess what David and Bathsheba named their third son? Nathan. Not only did David accept Nathan's rebuke, but he didn't hold a grudge. That's why God loved him so much."

I nodded, not sure what to say. I'd have to think about this some more.

"Well," John said, "I'm afraid I have to get these tires on. But while I work, I'll be praying for you."

"Thanks, John." I started out. "Oh, I almost forgot. My mom says I can keep Scruffy."

"Well, there's one answer to prayer right there. And he's looking good, too. There's another. You just relax. God's got everything in control."

I had to smile. "Yeah, John. Thanks."

That night, I took John at his words and relaxed. Dad and I played Ping-Pong and watched a hockey game together.

Sunday morning, I watched Charlie get into his car and take off for church, but I didn't go. When Mom asked if I wanted to go with her and Dad to visit my aunt in Stanton, I decided I may as well.

Later, I did some homework. At first I thought, why bother? If I wasn't going with Nicole, then it didn't matter what I did. But I immediately realized that was a dumb attitude.

Monday morning, I was early for breakfast. Mom was eating, but she started to get up to make me some toast. I told her to sit down.

"I can make my own breakfast." What was I saying?

She looked kind of surprised, but she sat back down. In a few minutes, I was sitting with her. As was Dad's habit, he had been gone for about an hour. He likes to get his paperwork done before people start coming in to talk to him.

Anyway, Mom and I finished eating and then got ready to go out. Mom had her coat on and was standing at the door when I came up.

She started out.

"Wait up, Mom," I said.

She looked surprised.

"There's no point in each of us walking alone."

I got my jacket and pulled my runners on without undoing them, and then we left together. I guess if I want to walk to school with my mom, I can. I mean, whose business is it, anyway?

We parted at the front door, she to the office and me to my locker.

Classes dragged, but noon came finally. I had brought my lunch, so I went to the cafeteria and sat beside Brett and Mac.

"So, how's it going?" Brett asked innocently.

"Fine," I said as I opened my lunch bag.

"That's not what we heard," Mac said, grinning.

"We heard you and Nicole had a fight," Brett said.

"Does anything ever happen in this town without every single person knowing about it?"

"Well," Mac said seriously, "my cat had kittens one night and the next morning nearly everybody I met asked me how they were."

"The answer is no," Brett said. "Everybody always finds out everything. Now you know what it feels like."

"Give me the city," I said, but I didn't mean it. There are a lot of good things about living in a small town, and at least people are interested in you even if they do carry it too far.

"I hear Nicole saw you with Marta," Mac said.

I refused to talk about it, so they gave up and we finished our lunches.

Then we went to the gym and played pick-up basketball. I'm not very good, but I still like to fool around.

After a while, Charlie and some other guys showed up and the game got a little more intense, so I cut out.

I decided to go for a walk.

But as I went out the front door, who should come up but Nicole.

Remembering what John had said, I called her name.

She stopped.

"We have a few minutes before class," I said. "Will you please just listen to me before you decide you don't want to be friends any more?"

# 11

Nicole looked first at me and then at her watch. Next she looked at me again, as if trying to read my mind. At last, she took a deep breath and said, "Okay, you've got five minutes."

She turned, and I followed. We walked to the corner of the school, where she leaned against the wall. "Okay," she said, "what do you have to say?"

"First, I like you very much. Second, I am not in any way, shape, or form interested in Marta Billings. Third, I did go to the movie, but if you don't think I should, I won't go again. Fourth..." I had no idea what was fourth. "Fourth, I—I think you're going to have to learn to trust me more."

She chose to respond to my last point. "I am?"

"Yes." I had no idea what I was going to say, but I plunged on. "I didn't think you were like the other girls, always getting mad and—and being—fickle, and getting jealous and all that stuff. If I—well, if I said you were the only girl I liked, and I did say that just a short time ago, then I don't see what right you have to go and get all upset just because you saw Marta acting like an idiot. Especially since I didn't do anything!

"I was just trying to defend myself from Marta and keep her from doing something dumb and getting into trouble. I have no idea what she's up to or why, but I did nothing to encourage her! But—" I concluded (probably the longest talk I'd ever given except maybe for a speech in grade ten) "—you aren't interested enough to bother to find out what I was doing. You listened to Charlie when you know all he wants to do is break us up, and you even spied—"

She tried to interrupt me, but I ignored her.

"Yes, *spied* on me, when you could have just come up to us and maybe even given me some help!

"And," I added grandly, "I got in this mess because I was doing what you wanted me to do—trying to help somebody!"

She met my eyes and then looked away. She spoke softly. "I know I reacted badly. I mean, it's not as if we're going steady or anything like that. I shouldn't have been upset. I just—well, somehow it never occurred to me that you might be dating anyone else and, well, I guess it bothered me a lot when I found out you were. Especially when you didn't tell me yourself. "

"I'm *not* dating Marta!" I exploded. "And I don't know why you still seem to think I am!"

"You went to a movie with her last Saturday night. You were with her Wednesday at Harry's. Glen, people saw you kissing in the middle of Harry's! Darlene saw you! I saw you on Friday myself!"

"I did go to a movie Saturday night."

She didn't respond.

"I went with Phil, Mac, and Brett."

There was a pause. "Not Marta?"

"There were no girls present."

"Not that it matters if you did go with her. Only—"

"I didn't and I won't! You know you're the only one I've gone out with."

"I heard you went out with Ann once."

"Only because Charlie set up a double date without telling me. Believe me, it was not a fun evening."

"Ann's pretty."

"There's only one girl I have ever wanted to go out with."

"Not—Marta?"

"Why on earth do you think I like Marta?"

"I've always thought you liked her."

I stared at Nicole. "You thought I liked Marta Billings?"

"Yes."

"Why?"

"You're always teasing each other."

"And I thought you were intelligent! Nicole, I can't stand Marta Billings, and the only kind of teasing she does has barbs attached to it. I can't believe that you could ever think I liked her!"

"Well, you've always talked to her more than you talked to me."

"I never dared talk to you before."

"Am I so scary?"

"No, I thought you were so far above me that you didn't even know I existed."

"Well, I did."

"I don't know why."

"Maybe I like the strong, silent type."

"I thought we were talking about why you liked me?"

"We were."

"I don't feel very strong, and if I'm silent it's because I never know what to say."

"What about last Wednesday? Why were you kissing her?"

"She phoned me and said she had to talk to me—that it was important. It turned out she wanted my help in getting Charlie to like her. And *she* kissed me. Took me completely by surprise. I had no idea she was going to do that."

"Friday?"

"She sat down in the booth beside me. You can ask Brett and Mac. I did nothing at all to encourage her. I don't know why she does any of the dumb things she does. I got away as soon as I could. She's crazy! I wouldn't go near her again if you paid me ten thousand dollars. Not even for ten million dollars!"

She looked down. "I'm sorry, Glen. I should have known better. I should never have believed the worst."

Then she began to laugh. I guess it was contagious, because I started to laugh, too. Suddenly, she grabbed my hand and held it against her cheek, and my heart just about flipped over.

"I'm sorry, Glen," she said. "And you're dead right. I should have trusted you. Wow!" She shook her head. "I can't believe I got so angry. I didn't think I was the kind of girl who went in for petty jealousy." She smiled ruefully. "Maybe it's because I've never really cared about anybody before."

"It's okay," I said quickly. "I just don't want you to be mad at me."

"I'm not." She was still holding my hand between both of hers. "Will you forgive me?"

"Sure." I was embarrassed now. "I'm sorry I got so fired up. I never meant to yell at you."

"I deserved it." Then she started to laugh again. "But if you could have seen yourself! Talk about righteous indignation! I had no idea you could get like that."

"I didn't either."

"I'm sorry I wouldn't listen to you before."

"Oh, that's okay." That terrible moment at her locker seemed like years ago.

The bell went just then. Still holding my hand, Nicole turned and started to run. We made it to class with only seconds to spare.

But I wouldn't have minded being late, even if I got a detention and had to go to the office. Nicole didn't hate me!

When classes ended, I got the books I needed to take home and hurried to Nicole's locker.

Charlie and Joyce were with her, so I hung back. Charlie was trying to get her to go to Harry's with him.

"Sorry," Nicole said as she put books into her locker.

"Aw, come on," Charlie said. He reminded me of a little boy begging for just one more cookie; only he was the kind of little boy who would grab two handfuls the second your back was turned.

"Can't," Nicole said as she continued to mess around with books.

"Just this once," Charlie begged.

"I'm busy," Nicole said, still not looking at him.

"You know you have to come with me sometime." Charlie stated this like it was a rule or something.

"Do I?" Nicole asked, her eyes wide as she finally looked up at him.

"Come on," Charlie said smoothly, "you know it's just a matter of time.

"Well, the time isn't now," Nicole said. She shut her locker and turned around. "Oh, there you are, Glen. Ready, Joyce?"

Both girls walked straight over to me.

Charlie's jaw dropped. "But I thought—"

Nicole smiled at him. "Did I forget to tell you that I found out you lied to me about Glen going out with Marta?"

"See you later," I said, and I have to confess that I grinned as I took Nicole's arm and the three of us began to walk away.

But you should never think you've got the better of Charlie. What did he do but run up beside Joyce and fall in step with her! "Hey, I've always heard that three's a crowd," he said. "How about it, Joyce? Do you really want to tag along with these two, or would you like some company?"

"So you can keep trying to convince Nicole to date you?" she asked.

"No," he replied, stretching out his hands, palms up. "I give up. I can't understand what she sees in him, but if she still wants him, she can have him. I just realized it's time I stopped wasting my time. I also realized I've been totally overlooking you. So how about it? Can I come along if I promise to devote myself entirely to you?"

What was Joyce to do? She's kind of overweight and not what you'd call a great dresser, and she wears her hair in waves that look sort of old-fashioned, and—well, she isn't bad-looking, but beside Nicole, she's just out-classed. To my knowledge she'd never had a guy interested in her in her whole life.

Let's face it, she didn't have a chance against Charlie.

She stammered something—I don't think even she knew what—and the next minute the four of us were walking two by two down the street to Harry's.

We found a booth and ordered fries and Cokes, and then just sat there, Nicole and I on one side, Joyce and Charlie on the other. I have to confess I was sorely tempted to stretch my leg out and kick him a good one under the table, but I restrained myself. If I did kick him, he'd probably find some way of getting both girls feeling sorry for him or trying to nurse him or something. You just never knew with Charlie.

"So, it's a beautiful day, huh?" said you-know-who.

No one spoke until finally Nicole sort of mumbled, "Yes."

"I take it you're going to the volleyball game Friday night?" Charlie asked.

Nicole and Joyce both said, "Yes."

I looked at them. I had no idea what they were talking about.

"Aren't you going to go, Glen?" Nicole asked softly.

"Yeah, Glen, aren't you coming?" Charlie looked at me innocently.

I fought down an insane urge to flatten his nose and looked at Nicole instead. "What volleyball game?"

"The one Mr. Reiss told us about last Sunday and again yesterday," she replied.

"Sunday?"

"At youth group."

"Oh."

"You were there, weren't you?" Charlie asked sarcastically.

"No, I wasn't. Not yesterday."

"I didn't notice."

"Yeah, right." I looked across the table at Joyce.

"Another church is coming to play against us," she explained.

"Oh."

"Are you going to come, do you think?" Nicole asked.

I wanted to ask her if she wanted me to go, and hear her say she wouldn't go herself unless I did, but all I said was, "Maybe."

"He wants you to talk him into it," Charlie said.

Fortunately, our drinks and fries arrived, so I didn't have to reply.

Joyce asked Nicole about something we had been assigned in history, and I used their conversation to mouth across to Charlie, "You rat!"

He just smiled his big innocent smile, and as I looked at that blond hair, and those blue eyes and even white teeth, I wondered why any girl in her right mind would want me when she could have him.

"Don't you think so, Glen?"

Ouch! Nicole was talking to me, and I'd been so deep in thought I hadn't even heard her! "I'm sorry," I said. "I was thinking about something."

"It wasn't important," she said.

"So, what do you all think of Mr. Reynolds?" Charlie asked. "With that red hair and the stuff on his face, all I could think of was a fox. Reynolds the Fox."

I didn't worry about answering. He wasn't talking to me.

"I guess he was okay," Joyce said after a minute. "He had very little chance to teach us anything today."

"He'll have to if old Jackman is away for any length of time," Charlie said.

"I hope he isn't," Nicole said. Then she got red. "I mean, if there's no help for his son, I hope he doesn't have to suffer too much. But, well, I don't know if he knows God at all, either, so—"

"So we really need to pray for him," finished Joyce.

Charlie didn't say anything, and for the moment I ignored his presence. With everything else that was going on, I'd forgotten all about Frank Jackman. "What should we pray for?" I asked.

"I think," Nicole said, "the best thing is to pray that God's will might be done in his life. God can always heal someone even if the doctors say there's no hope. But he doesn't often do that."

"But he might die without knowing God," I said. "Isn't the first priority that he gives his life to God?"

"So first of all we need to pray that he finds God, and then we can pray that God heals him if it's his will," Joyce said.

"I don't think anyone in the family knows God," I said. "We need to pray for all of them.

"That's right, Glen," Nicole said. She sounded pleased.

"Can you three lighten up?" Charlie complained. "All I asked was what you thought of Mr. Reynolds!"

"He's a teacher," I said as lightly as I could. "What more is there to say?"

Joyce sort of giggled, and Nicole smiled, and then we were talking about the basketball team and how Charlie was the star, and then we got back to the church volleyball game again.

I couldn't figure Charlie out. I knew the only reason he'd ever gone to church in the first place was to get Nicole interested in him, so why was he talking about going to the youth social? Unless he had lied about giving up on getting Nicole to date him. What am I saying? Of course he had lied!

And what about Joyce? Charlie had once used Marta to try to make Nicole jealous. Was he now going to pretend to be interested in Joyce so he could be near Nicole and me? And was there anything I could do to stop him?

We had finished our food, so we got up to go out. While we were paying, the girls walked outside.

"If you think you're going to use Joyce—!" I said quietly.

"Now, I thought it was Nicole you were interested in!" Charlie smiled at me as he spoke without moving his lips. "If you care to trade...."

"You know what you are? You're a snake!"

We had finished paying, so he turned and walked out. I had no choice but to follow.

Joyce was meeting her mother at the library. Sticking to his new role, Charlie went inside with her.

Nicole and I watched them go. I dug my fists into my jacket pocket. "For two cents—" I muttered.

"What did you say, Glen?" Nicole asked.

"I said for two cents I'd break every bone in his body."

"Well, I hope you don't think you have to try," she said practically, "because I don't think you'd get very far."

"Thanks."

"Come on," she laughed. "Joyce is no dummy. She can probably handle Charlie better than either of us."

I looked at her in surprise. "You think so?"

"I know so."

"But, I thought—"

"What? That because she doesn't have many dates, she'd be flattered to have Charlie's attention?"

"Well—yeah."

"Don't worry. When we were outside while you guys were paying, she was breaking up. She thinks Charlie is the funniest thing around."

"She thinks he's funny?"

"Like a little kid out to get his own way."

"Yeah, that's what I think, too."

"So don't worry about her."

"Okay," I said reluctantly. "But he isn't just a little kid. And he isn't funny. More like a snake."

"She'll be fine. Honest."

"I guess."

"Now, what about the volleyball game? Are you coming with us, Mr. Glen Sauten? Think what fun we'll have, you, me, Joyce, and Charlie." She went off into peals of laughter.

I didn't find the thought of going to the youth social with Charlie all that funny. It seemed to me I'd have to be on guard the entire time. But I didn't say that to Nicole.

Instead, I took her hand and we walked to her place, stopping at the vet's to see Scruffy. Nicole thought he was adorable. She also thought his name suited him. On the way home we talked about things a dog would need. Then we talked about the volleyball game. Like I've already said, I'm not much good at any sport that calls for fast reactions (which is most of them). But I said I'd try, and she was happy. So everything was okay again, and the whole business with Marta was history.

I dropped Nicole off at her place and went home. Mom was starting dinner.

"So," I said as I dumped my books on the table. "How's the job going? You still like it?"

"It's going very well, Glen. Of course, I've got a lot to learn, but I'm really enjoying myself. I think I'm going to like being there."

"That's good."

"How was your day?"

"Okay. Have you heard from the Jackmans?"

"I called Myra during my lunch break. She said Frank has been moved to a place called a hospice. They'll take turns staying with him. I wish there was something we could do to help, but there really isn't."

"Yeah," I said. But I felt guilty. Mrs. Jackman was one of her best friends, and maybe it would help if Mom were praying. Only from what Mom had said last night, I was afraid she didn't know any more about God than I had known a few months before. So maybe her prayers wouldn't help.

Maybe I needed to be praying for my own parents to come to know God—and for the rest of my family, too. I don't think any of them knew about asking Jesus into your life. They needed to know.

But who was going to tell them? Surely not me. Look at the mess I'd made with Phil. I needed to pray that God would send somebody else to tell them.

I went to my room and did just that. I even got down on my knees to make sure God had no doubt I was really praying in earnest. I prayed that Frank and all the Jackman family would come to know God, and I prayed that all my family would, too, and that God would send somebody to help them learn. Then, when I was about to stop, I realized that I needed to pray for Charlie, so he wouldn't be such a pain, and that he would come to know God. And that Phil would, and Mac, and Brett, and yes, even Marta. I also prayed that Joyce wouldn't get taken in by Charlie. Last of all, I prayed that Nicole and I wouldn't have any more misunderstandings.

By then, Mom was yelling at me to come for dinner. I looked at my watch and couldn't believe I'd been praying for thirty minutes. Ouch! But the truth was, I felt good—like I really had done something to help.

I hurried out to the kitchen to eat.

Dad was in a talkative mood. "So, I trust you haven't been bothered by your mother's presence at the school. Have the kids said anything?"

"No."

"They aren't teasing you?" Mom sounded worried.

I reached for more butter to put on my potatoes. "Mom," I said lazily, "I'm a senior. They aren't going to tease me because my mom's working in the office. And if they do—" I flourished my knife as if it were a sword, "—so what?"

Mom and Dad both looked at me, then at each other.

"Well," Mom said hesitantly, "I guess I won't worry about it, then."

"Of course not," I replied as I shoveled a forkful of potatoes into my mouth.

I spent the evening doing homework. I talked to Nicole on the phone for a while, partly to talk and partly to help me figure out what I was supposed to do in English. The assignment we'd been given made no sense to me at all until she explained it.

The next day went okay, too. Dad had left the car so Mom and I could pick up Scruffy after school. So I drove to school with her, suffered through classes, and a lunch with Charlie sucking up to Joyce, and met Mom at the car after school.

We went to the hardware store first and bought a kennel and a collar and bowls and a leash and food and a few other things dogs need. When we had everything in the car, we went to get Scruffy. First I wrote out a check for four hundred dollars. Mom thanked Dr. Clifton and said she knew that he hadn't charged the full amount. He said he couldn't take all my money. Then he let me go in and get Scruffy. The little guy nearly went wild when he saw me—his little ears pricked up, he started yipping, and his tail began to thump at full speed. As soon as my hands were close, he started licking them.

Carefully, following Dr. Clifton's instructions, I lifted him out of the cage and carried him to the examining table. Dr. Clifton showed us the incision and told us how to keep it clean. He showed us how the splint he had made for the leg worked. Using the splint, Scruffy could stand on the leg and take a few steps. So he could be taken outdoors and go to the bathroom and get a little exercise. The danger was that if he just lay there all the time, his muscles would atrophy.

Mom and I thanked Dr. Clifton and his staff and I carried Scruffy out to the car and held him as we drove home. Once there, we put him in his new kennel against the kitchen wall and organized the rest of his stuff. Within a few minutes, he was sound asleep.

"He seems contented," Mom said.

"Yeah."

"Glen, buying the things for Scruffy reminded me that when I was shopping Saturday I noticed some clothes at Parker's that I thought you might like. I was going to pick them up, but I wondered if you wanted to go there yourself."

"Clothes?"

"Now that you're dating Nicole, I thought you might like some new things."

I remembered what Nicole had said about her thinking Charlie might be a good influence on me. She obviously liked the way he dressed. Which meant she probably didn't like the way I dressed. I decided Mom was right. I should get a few new things.

Mom gave me a check and I drove back downtown. After thinking about Nicole and Charlie some more while I drove, I not only cashed the check but got money out of my bank account, too. I got a new winter coat, new jeans, and a couple of T-shirts, then added gray pants, a blue shirt, and a tie.

Mom and Dad seemed really happy that I'd bought the clothes. "Do you realize those are the first clothes you've ever bought on your own?" Mom said.

I wasn't exactly in the mood for this, but I made an effort, "Are they?"

"Well, if you don't count the Superman shirt you chose when you were five."

I smiled.

"I guess you're growing up, huh?"

If I was, I sure wished I'd hurry and get it over with.

# 12

I got Scruffy out of his cage and put the splint on him before taking him into the backyard to see if he needed to go to the bathroom. He seemed to know what to do. Afterwards, he took a few steps toward me and I picked him up and he yipped and licked and generally acted like a happy dog.

On Wednesday, I went home at lunchtime to look after Scruffy. He seemed to be okay. He wasn't biting at the bandages or anything. From his reaction when I walked in the door, he seemed to think I was the most wonderful person in the world.

After school, I asked Nicole to go to Harry's with me, but she and Paul and their younger sisters all had appointments with an optometrist in Stanton.

So I went home to look after Scruffy, and then went over to the hospital to see Phil. I wasn't sure what he'd be like. When I'd last seen him, he had told me to go back to being Charlie's friend and forget about him.

But he seemed to have forgotten all about that. In fact, he seemed glad to see me. Brett and Mac were already there when I arrived, and the nurse let me go in even though we were a crowd. Phil was sort of raised up in the bed a little and when I walked in, he said, "Yeah! Now we can have a game!" Turned out someone had given him a deck of cards and he wanted to play poker.

We played for about an hour before he got tired. I lost, of course. Luckily, we were only playing for pennies.

After dinner, John and Katherine and Mr. Smithers picked me up and we went to Pete and Colleen's house. They lived a little ways out of town—maybe a twenty-minute walk—in a dumpy little house surrounded by wrecked cars and assorted rusty machinery and tools—and of course his truck, which he used in his moving business. It was what my grandmother called an "eyesore." Fortunately, they lived on Screel Street and not the Main Street, so most visitors to town didn't go past their house.

Colleen seemed overjoyed to have us there. She had obviously tried hard to make the living room look nice, and she had baked chocolate chip cookies and made iced tea. She was all flustered over our coming. I wondered if they'd had visitors before. I think maybe just family members.

We shared what was happening in our lives, and looked at a couple of verses in the Bible that talk about how Christians need to grow. John said new Christians are a bit like new babies—they need older people to help them learn the basics. Just as a baby has to learn to walk and talk and eat good food and eventually read and write, so new Christians need to learn from more mature Christians how to pray and read the Bible and serve God. It made sense.

So from now on John was going to meet with me and with Pete for an hour a week each. Katherine was going to meet with Colleen and Mr. Smithers. Not that Mr. Smithers was exactly a new Christian, but he felt he was kind of rusty and wanted what he called a "refresher."

John gave out books for each of us to work on during the week. Then we would talk about them when we got together one on one. The book looked good. Practical, I mean.

I know I'd learned a lot when Pastor Grant and I had talked a few times after I first accepted Christ, so I knew it would be good for me to talk with John, too.

We prayed for about an hour and ate some more cookies.

As we were leaving, Pete said something about cleaning up the place some time, and I heard John and Mr. Smithers offer to help, so I did, too. Pete seemed real pleased. He said we'd wait till it was a little warmer outside.

Thursday went fairly quickly. Nicole and Joyce were busy with some sewing project, so Nicole went out to Joyce's on the bus after school and stayed overnight.

Charlie offered me a ride home, but I said I was going to see Phil. But when I dropped by the hospital, I discovered he was busy with some relatives who had driven up for the weekend to see him.

I decided to spend some quality time with Scruffy.

He was overjoyed.

Friday morning, I remembered the volleyball game that night and I wanted to stay in bed. However, I knew I had to go through with it.

At school, Nicole was friendly and Charlie was spending all his spare time with Joyce.

I had to pretend to believe him.

Charlie wanted to go for milkshakes after school, but Nicole said she couldn't. She had to get her homework done so she could go to the youth group tonight. Her family was going away for all day Saturday to some kind of conference for pastors and their families. So Joyce and Charlie went for milkshakes and I went to see Phil.

He was looking pretty glum when I arrived.

"Relatives gone?" I asked.

"They've been here all afternoon. Just went to have dinner and rest up. I could do without them, believe me."

I straddled the chair next to his bed. "Who's here?"

"My grandmother and my aunt and uncle and three cousins. They all feel sorry for me. I can't take much more of it." His face was pale and tense, like he'd been the other day with me.

"Tough," I said. "Are they going home soon?"

"Not until Sunday."

"Two more days."

"Yeah." We contemplated his misery in silence. "Know what's really annoying? Before the accident, they hardly even talked to me. I never thought they liked me at all. They don't like my father much. But now that I'm helpless, it's like they want to smother me."

"Maybe they were kind of scared of you before. I mean, you never have had much time for people you didn't like."

"Yeah. Now I have no choice. Even if I stop talking to them, which I do a lot, believe me, they just say how sorry they are that I'm not feeling well and blabber along. They'd never have dared do that before."

We were both silent for a few minutes, and then I realized Phil had fallen asleep. Likely exhausted from all the company.

I tiptoed out of the room and went home to play with Scruffy and work on the book John had given me.

Joyce had stayed in town after school, so at a quarter to seven, Charlie picked me up and we drove over to get her and Nicole. He acted like everything was wonderful. I didn't say much. What was the use?

When we got to the gym, Charlie started directing the whole thing. We were playing against another youth group from a town about forty minutes east of us. They weren't overly good at volleyball. Of course, they didn't have Charlie.

I played a bit, but we had enough kids without me and I knew I looked like a klutz out there. The only thing I'm any good at is serving, and even there I have a tendency to hit it too long. So I avoided going on whenever possible.

Nicole was okay. Not wonderful, but adequate. Joyce, like me, is better at applauding from the sidelines.

The games ended eventually. Mr. Reiss gave a short talk he called a devotional and then we ate pizza and root beer.

Nicole and I were with Joyce and Charlie, and most of the conversation centered on how good Charlie was at volleyball. They were joking and laughing, and I felt I might just as well be someplace else.

Then Nicole turned to me and said, "Why so quiet, Glen? Don't you think Charlie was fantastic?"

I mumbled something that must have sounded like a yes, because she turned away again, and started talking about the spin Charlie put on the ball or something.

Then some other kids came over and joined in.

I slouched in my seat wondering why on earth I didn't have more brains. I could have said no when they first started talking about my coming. Why hadn't I?

When they brought round more pizza, I dove into my fifth piece. For some reason, I was really hungry. But when I was through eating, I felt restless. Like I had to get away from Charlie before I did something stupid.

I went to the washroom and got the pizza sauce off my hands. After that, I stood looking in the mirror. Just who was Glen Sauten anyway? And how did other people see him? I looked perfectly normal—average—not good-looking, but not bad. Plain brown hair, a few muscles but not a lot, average height. Nobody you'd remember in a crowd. But did it matter how you looked?

I remembered the conversation I'd had with Phil about how Joyce might not be great-looking, but she was a nice person, and how Marta looked good but was poison. Dr. Clifton had looked like a grouchy old man but wasn't. What did people think of me when they met me? Unimportant? A nobody?

Pastor Grant had once said God loved me just the way I am. John talked about us all fitting into God's plan, like we were each specially made for some purpose. But what was God's purpose for me? I couldn't think of anything I could do for him that somebody else couldn't do a lot better.

And Charlie. Phil had said Charlie always comes out on top. But will he always? Maybe things aren't the way they seem. Maybe—? My head was spinning.

I left the washroom and stopped in front of Nicole. "Are you finished eating?" I asked.

She looked up at me as if surprised I was there.

"I feel like walking. Come on." I strode across the room, then turned and looked at her. She and Joyce and Charlie, along with a few others kids who'd been close enough to hear, were staring at me as if I'd lost my mind. "Are you coming?" I asked quietly. "If not—?" I looked at the door.

Nicole rose slowly and took a few steps toward me. Then she stopped and looked back at Charlie and Joyce. She looked at me again.

"Come on," I said.

By the time she reached the hallway, I had found our jackets and put mine on. I held hers out. She put it on, but very slowly, without saying a word.

After we were outside, that changed. "What is wrong with you?" she began. "That was rude!" Then her expression changed. "Are you sick? Is that why you went to the washroom the way you did? You don't look well."

"I'm fine," I said.

"But I don't understand—?"

"Let's walk."

She reluctantly followed me and we walked down the street with her a step or two behind.

"I take it you weren't having a good time," she said at last.

"Not especially."

"It would help if you weren't jealous of Charlie."

Maybe her saying that should have made me angry, but it didn't. Just tired. "I'm not jealous," I said. "I just get tired of listening to him talk all the time."

"You could have talked, too."

"I didn't have anything to say about the subject."

"We were only talking about volleyball."

"In case you haven't noticed, I'm not into volleyball."

"I think you're jealous because Charlie's so good."

Patiently, I repeated myself. "I'm not jealous. Just bored."

"I'm sorry if I bore you," she said in a small voice.

I stopped and turned toward her. "*You* don't bore me. I'd like nothing better than to spend the next year doing nothing but talking to you!"

In the street light, I saw her eyes fill with tears. "Oh, Glen, that's beautiful!" she whispered.

She came closer and I put my arm around her. We walked that way, slowly, with her leaning against me. We didn't talk a lot, just now and then, mostly about how the stars looked and things like that.

We walked about six blocks; then turned back. Since her house was across the street from the church, I was a little afraid of running into Charlie and Joyce, but although there were still cars at the church, Charlie's was gone.

When we got to her house, we stopped and she came back to reality. "Glen, I was only trying to help Charlie have a good time so he would see that God is real."

"Yeah, I know."

"You don't have any reason to be jealous of him."

I wanted to change the subject, so I asked, "Have you thought about the Jackmans at all?"

"Yes, I pray for them every night."

"I've been praying for them whenever I think about it."

"It's kind of scary, isn't it?"

"Yeah. Anybody, anytime... Do you think some things happen by chance?"

She shook her head firmly. "No way. God is in control. Even when we don't understand or we don't like the things that happen, God is still in control."

"Even when everything seems to be going wrong?"

"Yes."

"But isn't it hard to keep going through difficulties when you know God could fix them if he wanted to?"

"I guess. But mostly we have to keep trusting him."

I had a feeling I hadn't been doing very well the last few days. I had a lot to learn.

"Glen?"

"Yes."

"I'm sorry I was ignoring you tonight. I didn't mean to."

"That's okay. It was dumb of me to get upset."

"Charlie needs us to be his friends, Glen. He needs to know God—to know that being a Christian doesn't keep us from having fun."

"Yeah, maybe. Only that's not what he's thinking about. He's just thinking about you. The fact that you're a Christian is only an obstacle he has to overcome."

"But if we let him hang out with us, we have a chance to help him learn about God."

"You think he'll listen?"

"Glen, I feel really sorry for him."

"I still think you're wasting your time."

"So you want to forget about him? Not even try?"

I shrugged. "Suit yourself. I just don't think it'll do any good. But I've been wrong before."

"I'll think about it. You won't be mad at me if we double date another time? Joyce doesn't mind. I mean, she isn't crazy about him or anything, but she doesn't mind him."

"What about her parents?"

"Her mom's a Christian, but her dad isn't. Joyce talked it over with her mom, and she said it's okay."

"As long as Joyce knows he's just using her."

"She does. She couldn't believe it at first—that he would be so obvious about it—but she's willing to go along with it because she thinks we can help him."

I sighed. I'd long ago decided I'd never understand my sisters, so why should I try to understand Nicole and Joyce?

The only thing that really mattered was that Nicole wasn't mad at me. If she wanted to try to show Charlie he needed God in his life, well, I guess there wasn't anything wrong with that, was there?

"Okay," I said. "We can try."

"I'm glad we went for a walk," she said. "That was the best part of the night." She quickly kissed me on the cheek and hurried inside.

I stood for a minute staring at the door.

Then I wondered what Charlie was thinking right now. I had a feeling it wasn't anything positive. But I wouldn't worry about that tonight!

Wrong again! Wouldn't you know I was almost even with his house when his car came zipping up. He must have driven Joyce home in no time at all.

Charlie's brakes squealed as he pulled into the driveway and came to a sudden stop. He jumped out of the car and hurried straight across the street toward me.

I thought about making a run for my house. Maybe if I'd been ten, I'd have done that. But I'm getting too old to play hide and seek.

So I nervously stood my ground.

"Did you have a nice night, loser?" He was definitely annoyed.

"Okay," I said quietly.

"Yeah, sure. Look, I've had it with you. I've been Mr. Nice Guy, even going out with that drip Joyce so I could be around Nicole. But my stomach can't take this. I'm telling you for the last time—Nicole is my girl and I don't want you going out with her any more. Understand?"

Hands on hips, he glared at me, and I felt about six inches tall and made of Jell-O.

But I said, "She wants to go out with me."

He leaned closer. "Look, Phil isn't around to protect you any more. So what are you going to do, Glen? Want to find out? We could have it out right now. If I win, you stay away from her, and if you win, I do."

"She isn't a stuffed toy that you win at the fair. She has some choice in who she goes out with."

"Everyone knows it's really me she wants. So how about it, chicken?"

"You're really a jerk, Charlie."

"Starting to get mad, Glen? Hey, have you forgotten how mad you were because I hit that dog? Not mad enough to do anything about it, though, are you?"

That did it. I swung wildly at his head, but he laughed and ducked, and the next thing I knew his fist hit flush on my nose and the shock of pain washed over me.

He backed off and said, "Winner takes all, Glen. Winner gets Nicole."

I swung blindly and felt only air. He plowed his fist into my stomach and I doubled over. He shot an uppercut that caught my nose and jerked my head back. Before I had a chance to even figure out what to do, he had hit me again, this time on the jaw. My head snapped back and I went down hard on my back.

I rolled over, trying to get up, and he backed away. He wasn't even breathing fast.

I wiped my face. There was blood all over my sleeve.

"Had enough?" he taunted. I rolled onto my hands and knees and slowly pulled myself up to a standing position. "Well?" he said. "What do you think, loser?" I swung at his voice, but again I hit air. I took another one in the stomach and then he sent me flying backward onto the street.

"Hey, look at it this way," he said casually. "You had her over a month, so you can't say you didn't have a fair chance. And—" he laughed "—I'll bet you didn't even get to first base with her." Still laughing, he went into his house.

I lay for a minute wishing I could just seep into the asphalt. But of course, nothing happened. Painfully, I dragged myself to my feet and stumbled toward my house, praying Mom and Dad weren't home.

I actually had a prayer answered: there was a note saying they had gone over to the Trents'.

Scruffy was in his kennel asleep. I was careful not to wake him up.

I turned on the water in the bathroom sink and washed my face. My nose was bleeding, but although it hurt a lot, I didn't think it was broken.

I got cleaned up and changed into pajamas. Since Mom and Dad could be home any minute, I decided to go to bed so I didn't have to explain what had happened. Knowing Mom, she'd have me at the hospital if she saw me.

So I turned off the lights and went to bed. Every bone in my body hurt.

Not to mention every part of my mind. I now knew how it felt to get beaten up. Not to mention totally humiliated. I hadn't even touched him! And we'd been fighting over Nicole. How could I have been so stupid?

Still dwelling on the fight, I fell asleep.

Next morning was Saturday. According to my alarm clock, it was 10:30 when I woke up. The first thing I did was groan and turn over. I felt lousy and just wanted to stay in bed for the rest of the day.

"God," I said silently, "now what? I don't know if you've been watching, but things aren't going very well here. Phil is a mess; Charlie's worse than ever; and I'm not doing too well, either."

But then I remembered that Nicole wasn't mad at me any more and that Scruffy was doing fine. And Colleen and Pete were so happy. Maybe God was doing things after all.

But knowing that still didn't help me get up, or figure out what to say to my parents.

"Glen?" Mom's voice.

"Yeah?" Oh, great. Talking made my jaw hurt.

She opened the door a crack but didn't come in. Since the blind was drawn, the room was dark enough that she probably wouldn't be able to see me clearly. "Your dad and I are driving to Stanton to look for a new mattress for our bed. Anything you need?"

"No, Mom."

"Scruffy's been out and fed. He's asleep. You forgot to take him to your room last night, so we took him to ours. You must have been tired."

"Yeah, I was."

"Well, don't stay in bed all day."

"Okay. Have a good trip."

"We'll be back before dinner."

I relaxed against the pillow. A reprieve!

I got up eventually and had a look in the mirror. Not as bad as I'd expected. There were bruises and swelling on my left cheek and jaw, and some dried blood around my nose and mouth. But once I had cleaned up, the only noticeable problems were the bruises. I thought I would be able to explain them adequately.

I spent some time playing with Scruffy. Of course, he couldn't run or anything. But he loved having his stomach rubbed and pulling on a rope, which he could do while still lying down. I got dressed and took him outside for a while. He ignored the splint and walked around the yard as if he had always walked with that thing on his leg. He was getting better fast.

I felt weird. Like I had to do something, but I had no idea what. It was after twelve. I ate some cereal before trying to work on my assignments. I didn't get much done. It was as if I needed to do something physical. Go for a walk or something.

Nicole was gone for the day, so there was no point calling her. Phil would have his hands full with his relatives still around. I could have called Mac or Brett, but I didn't. I'd have to tell them what had happened last night.

Then I told myself I was behaving like a coward.

I talked myself into walking down to Harry's to get some food. No one stared at me. And the walk itself helped a bit.

However, it turned out chewing a cheeseburger was not the best thing for my jaw.

I was wondering how to eat when I heard movement. I looked up to see Lisa sitting down across from me. Now what?

In some ways, Lisa is the most popular girl in our school, although girls hate her and she drives guys crazy. I don't think she's ever spoken more than twenty-five words to me in her life, including the whole time she was going with Phil.

Today she was wearing a long black skirt, slit in the side, with high heels and a white blouse. She seemed to be going for a new look. She had dyed her short black hair a sort of burgundy colour, and she had on a lot of make-up, and long dangly earrings. She had a coat over her arm. She must have been sitting at another booth when I came in, and she'd spotted me as she was leaving. She looked as if she was on her way to a party or something.

"Phil's not doing too good," she said as soon as she was in the booth.

"Yeah?"

"It's a bummer. I hate seeing anybody like that."

"You've been over?"

"Yeah. A couple of times."

"Yeah, me too. It's hard to know what to say."

"You're telling me? I feel bad. You know, because of the Charlie thing. He's a creep, by the way. I could use a lot worse language than that to describe him."

"Yeah, I know."

"Phil asks me about you. How you're doing. I don't know much. Phil's worried that now he's out of the picture, Charlie's going to do something to you. I thought at least I should warn you not to turn your back on him. Although, from the looks of your face, I'd say maybe you didn't turn your back when you should have. Anyway, no matter what he might say, Charlie wants Nicole Grant, and that's *all* he wants. So don't trust him."

Some guy I didn't recognize came over to the booth. He looked older than the guys around here, and he was wearing a suit and a long coat. Lisa introduced him as Harv, a college guy from Stanton.

"Come on, doll," he said. "We should move it."

"I'll be with you in a minute, Harv. Guys!" she said to me as he wandered back to the counter. "Always in a hurry. Some fraternity party. Like anybody will care if we're late." She took her time getting out of the booth and smoothing her skirt. "Remember what I said, Glen. You play with fire, you get burned. Charlie is fire."

I thanked her, and she and her boyfriend left.

I picked up my cheeseburger with the works and took another painful bite.

"Waiting for me, sweetie?" Marta asked as she sat down beside me.

# 13

While instinctively moving over, I cringed inside. Now what?

"You know, you act as if you aren't completely thrilled to see me. What kind of attitude is that?"

"A realistic one."

She laughed. "Glen, when are you going to learn? Always give a lady what she wants."

"If I see a lady, I'll remember that."

"That was nasty."

"Tough."

"Why am I always getting the impression you really don't like me?"

"Why are you always hanging around if you have that impression?"

She cocked her head to one side. "You're getting downright talkative, boy."

I finished the burger as she ate my fries.

"So, whose fist did you walk into?" she asked with her mouth full.

"Your boyfriend's."

"Charlie's? As if I needed to guess. But when I saw him this morning, he didn't look as if he'd been anywhere near a fight."

"That's because *I* didn't hit *him*."

"Mmm. Did your dad never teach you how to feint and duck?"

I didn't bother answering.

"I could kiss your hurts and make them better."

"Don't bother."

"Why not?" She pouted. "What's Nicole got that I don't?"

"Why do you keep turning up wherever I go? And if you tell me you've suddenly fallen for me, I won't believe it."

"What do you want me to tell you?"

"The truth would be interesting. And novel, coming from you."

"You know, Glen, for a laid-back guy you can be as nasty as anyone, can't you?"

I looked down at my glass.

"Can you see my earring? I think I dropped it on the seat."

"If I find it, will you leave?"

"Wow, Glen, you're so much fun to be with. It's amazing!"

She started moving in the booth so she could see the seat. No earring. I bent down to see if it had fallen on the floor.

"Oh, here it is," she announced.

I sat up.

"I must have sat on it," she complained. "Can you fix it?"

I took the tiny earring from her. Sure enough, the part that went in her ear was bent. I straightened it and was handing it back to her when Joyce and Charlie walked in the front door.

I knew I was dead when I saw the look on Joyce's face just before she grabbed Charlie's arm and walked out.

Marta didn't seem to notice. She was acting like she was thrilled I'd fixed her stupid earring. But by now I'd had more than enough of this. I shoved her sideways and right onto the floor. Running outside, I was in time to see Charlie and Joyce drive off.

"I guess Charlie's won again, huh?" came an amused voice from behind me. "You didn't have to dump me on the floor. I would have moved if you'd said 'please.'"

I didn't waste my time talking to her. Just went back in and paid Harry and drove straight home.

I felt numb. I knew Joyce would tell Nicole she had seen us and Nicole would have a really hard time understanding my being with Marta again. How could I possibly explain? Every time I turned around, something else happened.

And then there was Charlie. What would he tell her about our fight? Fight! Doesn't it take two people to have a fight? Well, I sure hadn't done any fighting. There wasn't a mark on Charlie!

I turned on the TV and let Scruffy lay against me while I watched who knows what.

At three in the afternoon, I walked over to meet with John. We talked about the fight, and Phil, and then about the book he'd given me. I promised to start working on it a little every day. Then we prayed together for a while—mostly about Phil and Charlie and what I should do. And about Nicole, too. Afterwards, I felt a little better.

When I got home, Mom and Dad were back and they wanted to know about the bruises. I told them I'd slipped and fallen against the steps. I know it was a lie, and I know you're not supposed to lie, but although I had had no problem talking about it with John, for some reason I didn't feel like telling them Charlie had beaten me up and I hadn't even landed a punch.

We had dinner, and Dad and I played a few games of Ping-Pong. I lost worse than usual. After that, he helped me with my math. Finally, I took Scruffy outside and then carried his kennel to my room.

He'd been sleeping in his kennel at night, no problem. But tonight, as soon as I got into bed, he started howling. I took him out of the kennel but that didn't seem to be what he wanted. When I put him back in the kennel, he gave me a pitiful look and started howling again. Finally, I picked him up and set him on my bed. He immediately curled against me and went to sleep.

He slept like a log; I slept fitfully. I kept seeing Marta. She had a cup and she was pouring something that looked like blood out of it, and laughing wickedly. I seemed to be trapped in some kind of glass cage from which I could only watch her. Charlie and Nicole were in another cage, holding hands and laughing. Phil was in another cage, sitting on a chair saying, "I told you so." And all around us, watching, were other people—my family, Nicole's and Charlie's and Phil's families, John and Katherine and the others from the group, my teachers and classmates.... It was a relief when I finally woke up.

My body felt worse than it had the day before, but my head actually felt clearer. A couple of things had sort of clicked together in my mind somewhere in the middle of the night. I knew I couldn't just sit back and let things happen to me the way I had so often in the past. I knew that I had to keep trying to make things right, no matter what happened.

But I hadn't planned to start doing things at church that morning.

In the youth group session, Mr. Reiss had us looking up Bible verses about anger. We talked about how we shouldn't allow anger to control us or go on very long. All of which was good, except I felt as if it were a lesson from school—where you talk about the facts. It just didn't seem real, somehow.

It was Nicole's ignoring me when I first arrived and then sitting with Joyce and Charlie that got me going. Charlie, who beat me up one minute and acted like I was his best friend the next. Charlie was a fake, a phony.

Lisa had strengthened my belief that Charlie would do anything to get Nicole. But knowing that was one thing. Knowing what to do about it was another.

With all this going through my mind, I blurted out, "Shouldn't we do more than just *talk* about anger like it was something we could study? I mean, it's all theoretical—I think that's the word. Shouldn't we talk about real life? Like how many of us are feeling anger right now, and why, and what we're doing about it, and how we could help each other? Shouldn't we be praying for each other?" My voice cracked, but I kept going, letting my frustration out. "Shouldn't we get to know each other and not just say the words everyone wants to hear? I mean, what's the point of knowing what the Bible says if you don't do anything about it?"

There was a stunned silence in the room. Everyone was looking at me. Mr. Reiss was babbling something about following the lesson plan. Charlie was smiling and saying something out of the side of his mouth to Nicole and Joyce. I stood up and walked out.

No one followed. I had the car, so I went for a long drive. I got home about one o'clock, which was normal, so I didn't have to say anything to Mom and Dad.

I ate lunch and then went to my room and looked at the book John had given me. Today's lesson was about how our sin gets in the way of our relationship with God, but how he will always forgive us and let us start over again. I got down on my knees and told God how sorry I was for the way I kept messing up, and how glad I was he would let me start over. I remembered John's saying that new Christians are like new babies, and of course they make mistakes as they grow. But the funny thing was that I didn't know whether I had made a mistake or not. About what I'd said in youth group, I mean. It was likely the wrong time to say it and all, but what was right? Should we just talk about what the Bible says and not try to figure out how to deal with things? I mean, was it really okay for Charlie and Nicole and I to sit there and pretend nothing was wrong? Or should church be a place we could be honest with each other like we were on Wednesday nights?

I thought about talking to John, but I figured I already knew what he would say.

Maybe the person I needed to talk to was Pastor Grant. I prayed a bit more and then phoned him. He told me he had some free time and he would meet me at the church. I told Mom and Dad I was going out, and held my breath. But they didn't ask any questions.

Deciding I needed to release some energy, I ran the eight blocks.

If Pastor Grant had already heard something about my outburst, he didn't say anything. Just asked me to tell him what was bothering me. I was surprised at how easily it all came out. But I guess I trusted him. I had no reason not to. He had helped me find Christ in the first place, and he had also told me it was great that I was meeting with John. And he knew about some of the problems I'd had with Charlie.

So I told him everything—about Phil and Marta and Nicole and Charlie and Joyce, and how much I enjoyed the group Wednesday night and how frustrating I found the youth group and the other kids who were there, none of whom I really knew or seemed to have much in common with, except Nicole and Joyce. I told him roughly what I'd said that morning and why I'd said it. Then, exhausted, I sat back and waited for his reply.

"Glen, if you had to choose the person you know who most seems like Jesus would be, who would you choose?"

I didn't have to think about that. "John," I said. "And Katherine." Then, realizing who I was talking to, I added, "And I guess you, too."

He pushed his chair back and crossed his legs. "When John moved here and talked to me about the group he wanted to start, I urged him to go ahead. I was glad he wanted to reach out to people who didn't go to a church. I was glad when you got involved, too.

"You're absolutely right. There is a difference between that group and the church groups we have. Even the Bible study groups. Somehow, when the people of this church come together for the Learning Center after the worship service, or even for Bible studies, they get caught up in figuring out what the verses mean and forget about applying them to their own lives. Not just in this church. A lot of churches are like that."

"Do you mean—are you saying—was I really right? I mean, should there be more?"

"The problem as I see it, Glen, is that we've got a lot of Sunday Christians. People who come to church on Sunday and try to live fairly decent lives, but who don't really understand what it means to be full-time Christians. Either they're too busy or they don't really know how, or they just don't care. The real irony in this is that it's you, a two-month-old Christian, who had to point it out."

"It was because of John. I guess I thought everyone in the church should be like him. And you. Only they aren't."

"Not just aren't, Glen. Don't know how. To tell you the truth, I'm not even sure *I* know how."

"But you do. I mean, you cared about me."

"Only because you came to me, Glen. You were looking for answers and I happened to be handy. But how would I have ever reached you if you hadn't come looking for me?" He uncrossed his legs and sat up straight, staring at his desk. "Even today. When Aaron Reiss told me what had happened in the youth group, I knew I should talk to you. But it was you who phoned me, not the other way around."

"You would have," I said. "You would have done something."

"Would I?" He looked over at me. I had never seen him look so tired.

"So—" all of a sudden I wanted to get out of there "—you think I should keep going to John's group?"

"That's the only way you're going to grow," he said bluntly. "And you need to grow." His voice trailed off as he said, "We all need to grow."

I thanked him for his time and went home to try to concentrate on my homework.

At school the next day, the purple bruises on my jaw and cheek interested a few people. I told them what I'd told my parents—that I'd slipped and fallen against the steps. Most of the teachers and even some of the kids believed me.

Marta was hanging around when I went into the lunchroom at noon.

"You've always been a slow learner, haven't you Glen?"

"What's that supposed to mean?"

Marta snorted. There's no other word for it.

"And what about you?" I asked. "You seem to learn pretty slowly yourself. In fact, from the way you act, I'd say you should still be back in kindergarten."

Her eyes flashed angrily. "You're a creep, Glen Sauten. Did you know that? And I hope you never get your precious Nicole back."

Charlie was with Nicole and Joyce at lunchtime, and I saw them leave together after school. I went home and took care of Scruffy. Then I visited Phil.

He was really tired from having the relatives there and I didn't stay long. I think he was feeling pretty sorry for himself. He had sort of been a captive to all his relatives. I mean, he couldn't exactly leave the room, as he would have done a month ago.

"You'll get a wheelchair, won't you?" I asked.

"Like that'll help a lot. They'll be able to push me wherever they want."

"No, I think you can get one that you operate yourself. By buttons. So you could leave if you wanted."

"Yeah, sure. And go where? I can't drive my car. Not that I have a car," he said bitterly. "And how will I get in and out of the house? Or the school? It's hopeless!"

"No, it isn't. They'll just have to make some changes, that's all."

"Yeah, right. What do you know?"

I had to admit I didn't know much. And nothing I could think of saying made him feel better. If anything, he was more depressed when I left than he was when I arrived. But in another way he seemed better. Maybe he liked having someone to yell at. I don't suppose he could yell at his relatives.

Tuesday was dismal. I survived, but just barely. Charlie was gloating and Nicole and Joyce wouldn't even look at me. The kids from church gave me lots of room, as if I might bite or something. Only Mac and Brett seemed normal, and they were starting to talk a lot about summer jobs and what they were going to do in the fall, which I didn't want to talk about because that brought up the old college thing. My dad assumed I was going, but I really didn't have a clue what I wanted to do. So when Mac asked me to go to Harry's with him and Brett, I said I had work to do at home.

I played with Scruffy, did some homework, and prayed a lot about the whole situation. I also took the time to think about the dream I'd had Monday night and what Lisa had said Saturday, and a few other things, and I began to feel I was finally starting to see daylight. I knew there was only one person who could tell me the truth.

I didn't want to confront her at school. So after classes ended on Wednesday, I looked up Marta's address in the phone book.

When I got to her house, I was kind of surprised. Even though I've known her all my life, I don't ever remember being at her house before.

She only lives about five blocks from Nicole, but not in the new section where Nicole is. Marta lives in behind the railroad track in a kind of dumpy section of town. Not really bad, but not terribly good, either. The houses are some of the oldest in town, and they're mostly small bungalows with a few larger houses scattered around.

Marta's house turned out to be one of the bigger ones, with what looked to be three stories. But it didn't appear to be very well kept up. The paint was peeling, one of the windows on the third floor looked broken, the porch was sagging, and it just didn't seem to be a house people cared about.

I slowed as I got closer to the front door. What on earth was I going to do if Marta wouldn't talk to me? I stood at the door. There didn't seem to be a doorbell, so I knocked. No one came, but I heard voices inside. Loud angry voices.

A door slammed somewhere inside the house. I decided to leave. What was I doing running over to talk to Marta, anyway?

The front door opened.

"Looking for somebody? Or does Nicole have you in such a daze you don't know where you are any more?"

"Hi, Marta."

"Do you want something?"

"Yeah. I—I want you to tell me why you suddenly got so interested in me. Like phoning me to meet you and kissing me. I don't think you have any interest in me, so you must have had some other reason. I want to know what it was."

I heard a car but didn't see it. Anyway, how was I to know that one of Nicole's younger sisters had a friend who lived two houses down from Marta's house? Or that Nicole would have just picked her sister up.

Marta saw the car, though. She dashed down the steps to fling herself into my arms. I caught her because I thought she had slipped on some ice.

Nicole beeped the horn and waved to us.

As the car moved down the street, Marta disentangled herself and ran toward the door. "Sorry, Glen," she called. "It's too cold out here for me."

In that instant, when I realized Nicole had seen me at Marta's house with Marta in my arms, my whole life flashed before my eyes. My lips and tongue felt as if they were made of rubber. But I forced them to move. "Marta, you've got to tell me what's going on!" I yelled.

She laughed and shut the door. She really is a witch.

That night our group was meeting in Mr. Smither's small apartment, which was in basement of the building where John and Katherine live. Mr. Smither's opened the door the second I knocked, and apologized for having so little space. I had never been there before, so I was amazed to see the number of black and white photographs that literally papered every wall and filled every inch of three small tables, a large buffet, a bookcase, and a dresser. Apparently he'd been really into photography when he was younger.

The pictures were good, too.

They were mostly of people, but some were of inanimate things—buildings, cars, and stuff. I don't know anything about photography or art, but they looked really good to me. Interesting, I mean. John and Katherine had been there before, of course, but they thought the pictures were wonderful, too. As did Pete and Colleen when they arrived.

But later, as we talked, Pete said he felt funny with all those dead people looking at him. Kind of bothered him.

John used that to talk about a verse in the Bible—I think in Hebrews—about how the people who have died in Christ before us are watching and cheering us on, as if we were running in a race. Weird. I'm not sure I want people watching me—even dead people. Although I guess if God sees everything we do, what difference does it make if other people do?

We talked about that a bit, and then I felt I needed to tell them about lying to Mom and Dad and everybody about the fight. I did what John said was "confessed" that it was wrong to lie and said I wouldn't do it any more.

I left about nine and walked home. I was almost at my house, when I heard Charlie call my name.

I stopped and looked toward his place. He was sitting on his front step.

Just what I needed! I walked slowly across the street.

"So, how's it going?" he asked as I came up to him.

"Okay."

"Yeah? That's good."

"Did you want something?"

He actually looked uncomfortable. "Yeah," he said finally. "I wondered if we could talk for a minute."

I agreed, but only because it was easier than thinking of an excuse not to.

"Not here. Come inside."

I wanted to tell him I was feeling sick and had to go to bed, or I had homework I absolutely couldn't ignore any longer, but after my promise not to tell any more lies, I was stuck. I reluctantly followed him inside.

As usual, neither of his parents was around.

We went into the kitchen. "Want a beer?" he asked.

"No, thanks."

He got one for himself and a root beer for me, and we sat at the kitchen table.

"I'm not going to eat you or anything," he said as he opened his bottle.

"Huh?"

"You look scared."

"Do I?"

"Yeah." He took a long drink. "How's Phil?"

"Not too good. He can't walk, you know." I guess I sounded kind of sarcastic.

But he didn't take offense. Just said, "Yeah. Tough."

"I expect your dad can tell you more than I can."

"Sure he can."

There was a long pause. Charlie was staring at the table. It was almost as if he didn't know what to say, which was very unusual for him.

"Did you want something?" I asked finally.

"Sort of."

He paused for a minute and I wondered what excuse I could make to get out of there.

"About all the dumb things I've done—" he said finally "—I'm sorry." That wasn't what I'd expected to hear.

"Oh—uh—that's okay."

"No, I've been really stupid. You can't help liking Nicole."

I waited for him to finish.

"It's just, well, it makes me so mad that you have Nicole and you don't even appreciate her!"

"I appreciate her!"

"Yeah, sure." He sighed. "Maybe you just don't need her the way I do."

Don't ask me what made me say what I did next. Maybe I have this inner need to make a fool of myself. I don't know. But I said, "Your parents aren't around much, are they?"

He shrugged. "They're busy people."

"Yeah.

He took another drink, not looking at me.

"They don't have a lot of time for you."

"So?"

"So—" the words were coming from my mouth, but I had no knowledge of what I was going to say next. I just hoped that I didn't make him angry the way I had Phil. "So, I guess—I guess you need to know you're loved."

"I do, huh?"

"Yeah."

"And I suppose you love me, huh?"

I shifted in the chair, feeling as if I had on underwear that was three sizes too small. "Uh, well, that's not quite—"

"Oh, yeah, I forgot. God loves me. Right?"

"Yeah, that's it."

He picked up his glass and stared into it. "And all I have to do is believe that and everything will be okay, huh?"

"You've been to church. You must have listened some of the time."

"Yeah, I heard what was said. Some of the time."

"You have to do more than just listen."

He set the glass down and looked straight into my eyes. "What do I have to do?"

My brain was whirling. "You have to, uh, believe that you need God." I tried desperately to remember what Pastor Grant had said when he explained it to me just before Christmas. "God made us to be with him, but we blew it. Only he gave us a second chance. But we have to realize that we just make a mess of things when we do them on our own."

"What kind of things?"

"All kinds. I mean, like running your life."

"So I've made a mess of running my life. Then what?"

"You have to know that we can't do anything to earn our way to be with God, so that's why Jesus died. All you have to do is believe Jesus died to, uh, to pay for all the bad things we do, and ask him to take over your life, and he will."

"That's it, huh?" He drank some more, then picked up the bottle, turning it so he could see the label. "I just have to tell God I've messed up and ask him to take over?"

"That's it."

"Okay."

"What?"

"I said, 'Okay.'"

I stared at him, my mind blank. Was he really saying what I thought he was?

"So how do I do it?" His eyes drilled holes in mine.

# 14

"How do you—?"

"What you said. Tell him."

"Uh, we—uh, you close your eyes. Like to pray. And you just tell him you need him to take over."

"Can I do it right now?"

"I guess."

I stared at him as he shut his eyes and began to pray. Guiltily, I shut my own eyes.

"God," he said, "I guess I need you to take over my life since I'm not doing a good job. Is that it?"

I tried to remember what I had done with Pastor Grant. My mind felt fuzzy,I knew there was something about saying you were sorry. "Ask him to forgive you," I said.

"Please forgive me for—for what?"

"Uh, you know, for the things you've done that you shouldn't have."

"—for all the things I've done that I shouldn't have."

"And ask Jesus to come into your life to help you."

"Jesus, please come into my life and help me. Anything else?"

"Amen."

"Amen."

I looked at him as he opened his eyes.

"So," he said, "is that it? Am I a Christian now?"

"I think so. I mean, that's basically what I did."

"Good."

"You should talk to Pastor Grant. He knows a lot more."

"I don't think he likes me."

"Well, if you don't want to talk to him, I have a friend who knows a lot. He'd be glad to talk to you. He's been praying for you." Then I thought I should add, "So have I."

"Yeah?" He sounded surprised.

I looked at him. It was hard to believe these last few minutes had actually happened.

Then I remembered something else. "Have you got a Bible?"

"I don't think so."

"You need to get one and read it a lot. And you need to pray. The Bible is the main way God talks to us, and prayer is how we talk to him."

"It works?"

"Yes," I said with more confidence, "it does." I told him a little about reading the Psalms and about David and what I'd learned.

"Yeah, that sounds good. Well, if that's it, I guess I'd better get you back home."

"Yeah."

He walked me to the door.

"See you tomorrow," he said. "If you want a ride, I'll be leaving at eight-thirty."

"I'll see. Lately I've been walking with Mom."

"Oh. Okay."

"Well, good-night."

"Good-night."

I walked across the street to my house, wondering all the way if I should pinch myself to find out if it were all a dream. Had Charlie really asked Jesus to take over his life?

And then my brain got turned on again, and I remembered talking to Charlie in his car just before he'd hit Scruffy. He'd said, "I know her dad won't let her date me because I don't buy all that God talk." Had he become desperate enough to go through the motions of accepting Christ? Was this all part of his plan to get Nicole?

I remembered Lisa's warning not to trust Charlie for one minute. Was this just his latest ploy to steal my girl?

Not that she was my girl. She was through with me. And how could I blame her? After telling her to trust me, first Joyce sees me sitting beside Marta at Harry's fixing her earring, and then Nicole herself sees me in front of Marta's house with Marta in my arms!

And now Charlie had given his life to God. It was probably all he needed to convince Nicole to go out with him.

As I got ready for bed, I felt like the biggest fool ever. But I didn't have the foggiest idea what to do about it.

The more I thought about it, and about how easy it had gone, the more I felt certain that it was simply his latest battle plan. But what if it wasn't? What if Charlie was on the level?

As I lay there, with Scruffy snuggled against my legs, I started talking to God. But this time, after I'd told him all my problems, I just lay there quietly, giving him a chance, if he wanted, to respond.

Suddenly thoughts were coming into my mind. Nothing fancy, but first the feeling that he loved me, just as I am. Then something that sounded like a Bible verse, though I didn't have a clue where it was found. I think I'd heard it somewhere before. "Worship the Lord your God, and him only shall you serve."

What is worship? I wondered. Wasn't that what we did on Sunday when we sang songs and listened to the sermon? Or was there more to it? And what could I possibly do to serve him?

The next morning at school, Charlie hung around me as though we were handcuffed together.

Nicole, except for looking at me once, ignored me.

At lunch, Charlie said, "So, have you told the girls about me yet?"

At first I didn't have a clue what he was talking about. When I remembered, I shook my head.

"Let's go tell them."

I followed him to the music room where Nicole was playing the piano and Joyce was singing. They sounded good.

"Do you mind if we interrupt for a minute?" Charlie asked when they finished the song.

"What do you want?" Nicole didn't sound thrilled to see either of us.

"We won't keep you long." He flashed her that endearing grin that seemed to make every other girl weak at the knees. "Just wanted to tell you what happened last night."

"I'm sort of busy right now," Nicole said.

"What happened?" Joyce asked with slightly more enthusiasm.

"Well, Glen here helped me do something I should have done a long time ago. I—er, how do I say it, Glen?" He looked at me.

"You asked Jesus into your life." My voice had about the same level of enthusiasm as Nicole had just shown.

But Nicole's face lit up and Joyce shouted, "You did?" Then they both hugged him and generally made like they were happy.

"That's not all," Charlie said. "I know I have to start all over again. And be truthful. So that means I have to tell you about some things I did that were wrong."

He had our attention.

"I guess you know I told Nicole Glen had gone to a movie with Marta."

We nodded.

"But I bet you don't know I paid Marta to make it look like she and Glen were together."

"You *paid* Marta?" Nicole asked in disbelief.

"I'm afraid so. We staged things so you'd think Glen was two-timing you." He shrugged. "I hoped you'd ditch him."

"Charlie, that's despicable!" I had never heard Nicole sound so enraged.

Charlie hung his head. "I knew it was wrong, but I was desperate. But I'm really sorry." He looked up and sighed. "I'm sorry I beat Glen up, too."

Nicole glanced knowingly at me. "So you didn't fall."

"I'm sorry Phil got hurt, too. I wanted to beat him in the race, but I didn't plan for him to get hurt. I feel awful about what happened."

There was a momentary silence, which he broke. "I'm sorry about the dog, too, Glen. Nicole told me how you took care of it. I'll pay you back whatever the vet cost."

All three of us stared at him. This really didn't sound like Charlie. Could I have been totally wrong in my suspicions? Had he been on the level last night?

"As you pointed out, Glen," Charlie said quietly, "my parents aren't around much." He was staring at the floor, moving his foot as though it were doing some kind of technical drawing. "I really don't have anybody who cares about me. My parents sure don't, anyway."

Nicole and Joyce were both close to tears now. They hugged him and told him they cared about him and they'd forgive him and help him learn and grow.

"And Glen will too. Won't you Glen?" added Nicole.

"Yeah. Yeah, sure." My voice was hoarse.

Nicole came toward me. "Oh, Glen," she said, "I'm so sorry. When Joyce told me you were with Marta again on Saturday, I was so angry. And then yesterday when I saw you with her—"

"Yesterday?" Charlie asked.

"I guess you were paying her," she said.

"No. I only paid her once. Well, then, there was the other time. She did something and then asked me to pay her afterwards. But that's it."

Nicole looked from me to Charlie and back. She started to say something, but just then kids began coming into the room for a class, so she stopped. This was no time to get into a long discussion of my relationship with Marta.

Nicole and I agreed to go to Harry's with Charlie after school so we could talk more. Joyce reluctantly said she had to go home, even though Charlie offered to drive her there later if she stayed.

At Harry's, I spent a miserable hour with Charlie and Nicole. She was all bubbly—thrilled that he had accepted Christ and that he and I were back to being friends again. I wished I were invisible. It was impossible to talk any more to Nicole about Marta. That would have to wait.

Nicole finally said she should go home because her mom wanted her to do some stuff. She climbed in the back of Charlie's car and I got in the front. At her house, I jumped out to help her. As she got out, she said, "Glen, we need to talk."

"Yeah, I know. But it's waited this long. I have to go and see Phil tonight."

"I'll keep?" she asked.

"He won't," I corrected.

"Can I go with you?" Charlie voice intruded.

I stared at him.

"I need to make things right with him."

I felt dazed. "You what?" I said.

"Oh, Charlie, I'm so proud of you," Nicole gushed.

"I'd like to talk to Phil," he said to me.

Regaining my brains, I shrugged. "It's a free country. I don't know if he'll see you or not."

"I don't see why he wouldn't," Nicole argued.

I looked at her. "Well, if you expect Phil to be thrilled because Charlie's accepted Christ, you'd better think again."

"Glen, you're not being very helpful to Charlie."

"Sorry."

"Aren't you feeling well?"

"I'm okay."

"Well, I hope Phil has the sense to talk to you, Charlie. Glen, I guess I'll see you when you have the time."

Charlie drove home without talking. I guess I had been pretty curt to him and Nicole.

When he had parked in his driveway, he asked again about visiting Phil with me. I had had a little time to think it over, and I just said that if he thought he should go, to go ahead, and I might see him there. He didn't argue.

Fortunately, Dad and Mom didn't need the car after dinner. I spent a few minutes with Scruffy before heading out to the hospital.

Phil was lying there watching TV.

We made some small talk before I asked, "Have the doctors decided anything yet."

"They're sending me away on Monday. Rehab."

"No change?"

"Nothing."

"How long will you be gone?"

"I don't know. A month. Maybe more."

"What about school? How will you pass?"

"Oh, I can do the work okay. They'll bring me books, and they'll even have someone come in and tutor me if I want."

"You should do it. You don't want to lose the year."

"Well, if I stay like this, it won't matter much, will it?"

"You won't, Phil."

"That's easy to say."

"I'm not just saying it."

"Yeah? Well, thanks. So, how is everything going?"

I was about to answer when someone walked in.

We both looked over to see who it was. Charlie.

"Phil. Good to see you." His presence filled the room.

As Charlie came toward the bed, I left the chair I'd been sitting on and moved away.

"So—" he said.

"Yeah," Phil answered.

"Tough luck," Charlie said.

"Yeah."

Charlie cleared his throat. "You know I never intended anything like this."

"Yeah, I know."

"So, how much longer are you going to be out of circulation?"

"Not sure. I have to learn how to use a wheelchair, I guess."

"Can't they do something to get you walking again?" Charlie's voice was impatient, and I realized what a hard time he would have if he were in Phil's shoes. Ouch. Not a good analogy.

Phil shrugged. "Not at the moment."

"Well," Charlie cleared his throat again, "I just wanted to come by and tell you how sorry I am this happened." His speech sounded memorized. "I hope you can forgive me for making you race me."

"You didn't make me do anything!" Phil said impatiently. "Racing you was just as much my idea as yours. And you pulled me out of the car, so I should be thanking you I'm alive."

"So can we end this fighting we seem to do all the time?"

"Yeah, it's over," Phil said.

Charlie shoved his hand in front of Phil's face and Phil shook it.

"No hard feelings?" Charlie said.

"No," Phil said grimly.

Charlie grinned. "Well, I hope you get out of here soon." And he was gone.

I slowly came back to the chair next to the bed and sat down.

Phil was still watching the door as it slowly shut behind Charlie. "I'm glad that's over," he said after a moment.

"I am, too. I hope it stays over."

"When you can't walk, you don't worry too much about who can run faster," Phil said quietly. "Don't know why I ever thought I could top good ol' Charlie. I doubt if anyone can."

I nodded. Yeah, one way or another, in the end Charlie always landed on top.

I thought of his campaign to get Nicole, and wondered again if what had happened was real or just the latest move.

Since it was only 8:30 when I left the hospital, I decided to drive over to the Grants' and see if Nicole was able to talk.

"Can we go for a drive?" I asked when she appeared.

She looked me over. "I guess so." She put on her coat and boots and found gloves.

As soon as we got in the car, she said, "You didn't seem very enthusiastic about Charlie."

I concentrated on driving, thinking about where to go.

"Glen?"

"Yeah?"

"I asked about Charlie."

How did I phrase this? "Well, I just—I just don't know."

"You don't know what?"

"Whether—whether he really did."

"What do you mean?" She gasped. "Glen! You think he's pretending he became a Christian, don't you?"

"Well—"

"Glen, how can you even think such a thing? Charlie would never do that—would he?"

"I don't know."

"But why?"

"You know why."

"Because of me?" She was really horrified now.

I nodded.

"But—but you were there, weren't you? Charlie said you told him what to do."

"I know. And he did it. I mean he said what I think you're supposed to say."

"But you think he might not have been serious?"

"Well, I wouldn't put it past him. He knows your dad doesn't want you dating non-Christians."

"You really believe he would fake it?"

"Yeah, I'm afraid I do. But I hope I'm wrong."

Her eyes filled with tears, and one fell onto her cheek. "I don't understand how you can think that," she said. "I'm sure he's sincere. Look at how he told us about paying Marta! And he wanted to see Phil. Do you dislike him so much that you won't let yourself believe he could change?"

I looked at her for a long moment. Finally I said, "Maybe I should take you back home."

"Maybe you should."

I started to turn the car, but thought better of it. "No," I said, "we have to have this out. You saw me at Marta's yesterday."

"You were hugging her."

"No, I wasn't. She jumped at me. After she saw you."

"Why were you there?"

"Because I had some crazy idea of getting her to tell me the truth, which we now know. Charlie was paying her."

"I guess."

"You guess?"

"Well, he said he only paid her once. Or maybe twice."

"I guess you'll have to decide whether you believe Charlie or me."

"Why have you changed so much, Glen? You don't seem like the same person I knew before. You're always angry."

"I'm not angry."

"What then?"

"Oh, I don't know. There are a few things bothering me. Other than Charlie, I mean. For one thing, I guess I don't like your always telling me off."

"What do you mean?"

"Well, in the last few weeks you've told me I'm lazy and not that bright and not as nice as you thought I was, and rude and untrustworthy. Just now you told me I'm always angry."

"Have I really said all those things?"

"Yes."

"I never realized—I'm sorry."

"Aw, it's okay. They're likely all true. Only...."

"Only what?" she said when I didn't continue.

I decided to tell her what I was thinking no matter what the consequences. "Well, I thought a girlfriend was supposed to tell you how great you were, not how many things are wrong with you! Sometimes I wonder why you go around with me at all since you don't seem to like me the way I am."

"Glen, I do like you the way you are. I guess, well, I guess I shouldn't say whatever I think, only—I guess I sort of felt that I could say anything to you. I thought I could be honest and not have to pretend."

"Well, can't you find something good to be honest about once in a while?"

She began to laugh. "Yes, I can find all kinds of good things. I just didn't realize I needed to."

"I'm likely being dumb. But it seems as if you're always finding things to complain about with me, and then sticking up for Charlie no matter what he does."

"Only because I feel sorry for him."

"I feel sorry for him, too, but that doesn't mean I have to trust him, does it? What if he is faking all this Christian business? I know you don't think he is, but what if he is?"

"If he is faking it, he's asking for trouble. It's not a game, Glen. It's God he's messing around with! The Bible says that God is worthy of our worship and adoration. And he is jealous of his place in our lives. He doesn't take kindly to people who use his name and his authority for the wrong purposes. If Charlie is crazy enough to fake something like this, he is in real trouble."

"Charlie doesn't realize all that."

"Maybe, but he'd still be playing with fire."

"I guess I hadn't thought of it that way. What should we do?"

"If you really think he's faking it, you should warn him."

I don't know. Maybe it's better for Nicole to see me as somebody whose faults need to be pointed out. Because when she starts to think I'm capable, she expects me to do stuff that's totally impossible. Couldn't she find some kind of middle ground where I might be able to stand up?

And why did Charlie seem to be continually in my face? First, with his threats, then paying Marta to get Nicole angry, then using Joyce to stay around Nicole, and now this! I finally understood the urge Phil had several times obeyed to go and knock him down. Well, in my case, *try* to knock him down.

We talked a bit more, and then I drove her home. Somehow our conversation was flat. It was as if Charlie and Marta were sitting between us.

When we got to her house, I had a sudden impulse. "Do you think your dad would have a minute?" I asked.

She gave me a surprised look, but nodded. "He was playing chess with Paul. Come in and I'll see."

A few minutes later, I was sitting with Pastor Grant in his study. The last time I'd seen him, he'd looked really tired. Today, he looked the way he usually did.

He smiled as he said, "So, anything in particular on your mind, Glen?" He leaned back in his chair. "Want my advice on how to get along with my daughter?"

# 15

I tried to laugh. "I don't know. I'm sort of mixed up. Did Nicole tell you about Charlie?"

"She told me that he had accepted Christ and you didn't seem to be very happy about it."

"I just don't know if I believe it!"

"So you think he would fake it?"

"I think he'd do just about anything to get Nicole."

"I see. So you have a dilemma. If you confront him, he'll simply deny it; if it happens to be genuine, your confrontation could push him away. Could be you'll have to let things take their course."

"You mean wait and see what happens?"

"Yes."

"That's funny! Before, that's what I always used to do. It's only since I became a Christian that I've been trying to make things happen. And I seem to make a mess of everything I try." I told him about Phil, and how I'd blown it with him. And how Charlie had accepted Christ without any apparent reason—at least not one I liked.

"You never know, Glen. Don't underestimate the Holy Spirit. Don't feel bad that you overdid it with Phil. As long as he'll still accept you as his friend, just show him love without saying anything. A lot of people are in positions where they can't say much, but they can always show God working in their own lives, and the Bible says it's possible to win someone to Christ without a word."

"So just be his friend and not tell him about God?"

"For now. He really needs a good friend. He's going through a terrible time."

"Yeah."

"As for Charlie, I told Nicole that I'd try to talk with him. Do you think that's a good idea?"

"Yeah."

Boy, did I! If Pastor Grant talked to him, maybe Nicole wouldn't expect me to!

"So I can find out if he's faking?"

I looked down. "I know what you're thinking," I said.

"Do you?"

"You think I don't want it to be real."

"Why would I think that?"

"Because if he were a Christian you'd let Nicole go out with him."

"You're afraid that she would?"

I shrugged. "All the girls are crazy about him. Given a choice of him or me, why wouldn't she want him?"

"I thought it was you she liked."

"Right now, I don't think she knows herself." I leaned forward. "It's not that I care. I mean, she's welcome to go with him if she wants. Only—"

"Only?"

"I don't know. I wouldn't want her to get taken in."

"So you're hoping I can prove he's faking it?"

"I don't know," I said, trying to be honest. "I don't think so. I mean, I think I would like it to be genuine. I'm just afraid it isn't."

"Are you and Nicole still having problems?"

"She's got me so confused. She says she doesn't like Charlie, but she's always talking about him. She seems to like having him around. She doesn't even seem to mind his using Joyce to hang around her. We've had a couple of what I guess were fights, and then we've made up after. But I just don't understand her."

"I think Nicole is the first girl you've been interested in, isn't she?"

"Yeah."

"Well, you're not the first boy she's dated, but you are the first one she's been in any way serious about. I think maybe she's as puzzled about the relationship as you are."

"I really do like her."

"Yes, I know you do.

"But—I guess I used to think she was perfect."

"That's because you didn't know her well enough."

"Maybe—but I still think she's the nicest girl I know. Easily. Only I don't always understand her. I'm never sure I'm doing the right things. Sometimes she gets annoyed with me."

"Has anybody ever told you that women are hard to understand?"

"I do have three older sisters."

He laughed. "Well, you shouldn't need to be told." Then he got serious and leaned forward on his desk. "The best advice I can give you, Glen, is to try to follow Jesus' commandments."

"You mean to love God?"

"And your neighbor as yourself. Yes. What I mean is for you to always put God first, no matter how important the relationship with the girl might be, and then to treat her in the best way you can—the way you'd like to be treated—even if it isn't the best for you."

"You mean do what's right for her even if it's not what I want to do?"

"Yes. I know that's a lot easier to say than it is to do. But if more people would do it, we'd have a lot fewer problems in the world."

It was my turn to nod. Then I made what was for me a profound statement. "God's way isn't ever the easy way, is it?"

He laughed again. "Not often. But it's always the best."

We talked a bit more. He asked me how things were going in the rest of my life. He encouraged me to keep spending time with John and meeting with his group.

"John has my blessing. I wish I could get my whole church meeting in groups like that. However, I know I couldn't just tell them to do it. But I'm happy for anyone who joins them."

Then he prayed for me, that I would have wisdom to always choose the right way, and I went home to bed.

I prayed for a while, and then I turned the light on and got out my Bible and found the book called First Samuel. That's where the story about David is.

I read the story about the giant Goliath again. When David first said he'd fight Goliath, everybody made fun of him. Well, why not? Here he was, just a nobody, thinking he could fight single-handed against the toughest guy in the enemy army! I would have thought he was crazy, too.

Only he can't have been crazy. Because he won.

It took me a while to figure out why he wasn't crazy, but at last I thought I found it. He was defending God. The enemy army had taunted God, and none of the Israelite soldiers had enough faith in God to believe that God would help him win. David was the only one who believed. So it wouldn't have mattered if David had been a skilled warrior or a six-year-old—it was God who decided who was going to win that fight because it was God's honor that was at stake. Because David loved God, he realized that.

But just because he loved God didn't mean he always had it easy. He made mistakes and he had a lot of hard times. But he kept trusting God, and God used him as an example of the kind of person he wants us all to be. So I prayed that God would use me the same way and went right to sleep.

Saturday dawned clear and bright.

Mom wanted some help around the house, so I spent a couple of hours going through some junk in the basement—old games and puzzles and stuff—and throwing a bunch of it out. I also spent some time with Scruffy. He was getting stronger every day. Next week he had to go back to Dr. Clifton to have his leg checked out.

Next on my list was Phil.

His mom was there when I got to his room, but she immediately left so I could visit.

"So," he said.

"Yeah."

"Turns out they're moving me tomorrow morning."

"Really?"

"Yeah. So they can start their tests first thing Monday."

We talked for a while about all kinds of things—school, the kids, Marta, Charlie, Nicole. I finally told him about Scruffy. At last we were kind of all talked out.

A nurse brought in his lunch. "You need to go to physio right after lunch." She gave me a look that said I was definitely in the way.

"I guess I should let your mom see you," I said.

"It's okay. She's going with me. They're letting her have some time off work."

"That's good. Will your sister be okay?"

"Yeah. She's got a friend she can stay with when Dad's not there."

"Oh."

"Well, I guess I'll see you some time."

"Yeah." I took a deep breath. "Phil, I know you don't like the God stuff, but—well, I'll be praying for you anyway."

He shrugged. "I don't suppose it can hurt."

"No. "

Not knowing what else to say, I started to leave. "Glen?"

"Yeah."

He swallowed hard and then gritted his teeth. "I'm scared, Glen."

"Yeah," I said. "I would be, too."

"Don't tell anybody."

"I won't."

Sensing I needed to do something more, I walked over and gave him an awkward, hesitant hug. His arms almost crushed me. After a second, he let go and turned his face away, but not before I had seen the tears in his eyes. "I must be getting soft," he said jerkily. "I've got to get out of this place."

"I'll write or something."

"Huh! I'll believe that when I see it!"

After that I knew I had to go and talk to the last person I wanted to talk to. I'd even prefer to spend time with Charlie.

When I knocked on the door this time, an old lady answered. She had a strong accent but don't ask me what it was. German or Russian or something like that maybe.

I asked for Marta and she opened the door to let me inside the house.

She went to the bottom of the stairs and yelled Marta's name before disappearing into the kitchen.

Eventually Marta came down the stairs from the second floor. As usual, she was in black, this time a caftan that looked like a monk's robe. She had on black bedroom slippers, too. She had apparently just washed her hair because it was rolled up in a green towel.

"What do you want?" she said from where she had stopped halfway down the stairs.

"We need to talk."

"Nope." She started back up the stairs.

"Marta," I said.

"Not interested."

"Charlie told me," I said. "And Nicole and Joyce know, too."

She paused. "Told you what."

"The truth. How he paid you."

She came back down a step or two. "Well, you didn't really think I'd kiss you without being paid, did you?"

"I have to confess I didn't think even Charlie would stoop that low."

"But I would?"

"You seem to have a way of doing nasty things."

"I try hard. Especially where you're concerned."

"Charlie says he didn't ask you to go to Harry's on Saturday."

She tilted her head to one side. "No. That was on me. Because of how you were always mean to me. I saw Charlie parking his car outside, and realized Joyce was with him. So I just ran in and threw myself into your arms.

She smiled, but it wasn't a nice smile. "Some of it you brought on yourself, you know. The first time was Charlie's idea, but afterward I got cold feet. That's why I called you. I was going to tell you the truth. Only you wouldn't meet me and you were nasty. So I decided you were getting what you deserved. When I saw you going into Harry's with Brett and Mac, I called Charlie and told him to see if he could get Nicole over there in a hurry. So you see, if you'd treated me differently, most of it never would have happened."

I digested that.

"Anything else?" she asked, her towel-wrapped head tilted to one side.

"I don't understand why you would help Charlie. You found out before Christmas that he was just using you to make Nicole jealous. You were angry enough to slash all his tires. Why would you then turn around and help him?

"I guess I'm not particular who I get money from."

"I guess not."

"Or maybe I have other plans of my own."

"I expect you do."

"Anything else you want explained, little boy?"

"No, I guess not."

"Charlie really told you about paying me?"

"Yes." He could explain why to her himself.

"So, you want to give me a kiss to make up?"

"Yeah, right," I said as I ducked out the front door.

I drove home and phoned Nicole. She agreed to go for dinner with me tomorrow night.

After supper, knowing I couldn't put it off any longer, I wandered over to Charlie's.

Dr. Thornton was actually home. He had on a T-shirt and he was holding a beer as he read the newspaper. For a fleeting moment he reminded me of Phil's dad.

Charlie and I went up to the room he shared with all the latest technological entertainment equipment. He put a CD on so we could talk without being overheard.

"I'm glad you came over, Glen. I needed to talk to you, and I don't quite know how to say this."

"Say what?"

"Oh, well, I guess about Nicole and me."

"Nicole and you?"

"Well, you know I couldn't date her before because her dad won't let her date anyone who's not a Christian. Now that I am one...." His voice trailed off.

"Now that you are one?" I prodded.

"Well, do you mind if I ask her out? I mean, it isn't as if you two have said you wouldn't go out with any other people, is it?"

I sighed. "No, we haven't said anything like that."

"So, am I free to ask her out?"

I remembered what John had once said about letting other people make their own decisions. Whether or not Nicole dated Charlie wasn't up to me. "Yeah, I guess."

"You don't mind, do you? I mean, she can always say no if she wants to, right?"

"Yeah, right."

"So, no hard feelings?"

"No."

"Good. I wouldn't want to do anything to spoil our friendship now that we're back where we were."

"Yeah." Where did this guy get off, anyway?

"You're sure, Glen?"

"It's okay."

"You came over here. Did you want something?"

"No. I think we've covered it."

I went back home and spent the rest of the evening actually getting some assignments done.

In the morning, I did some stuff for mom and worked on an essay I had to write.

I met with John in the afternoon, and that was good as usual.

At six-thirty, I picked up Nicole and we went to the hotel for dinner. I wore the new clothes I'd bought, tie and all. During dinner, we talked about school and other people and anything except Charlie.

Afterwards, on the way from the car to her house, she nearly tripped over her scarf. "Watch yourself," I yelled as I grabbed it.

She laughed and caught my arm.

Her face was a few inches from mine, and as I saw her in the glow of the streetlight I had to catch my breath. She really was something. Her eyes were sparkling, her smile enchanting, and her laughter delightful. She was Cinderella at the ball.

And I was Glen Sauten, with no blue blood whatsoever.

"I really enjoyed tonight," she said.

"Yeah," I answered, but my voice was hoarse.

"What did you say?"

"I said it was great."

"Except we kind of skirted around a few things. I—I wanted to tell you, but I didn't know how. My dad talked to Charlie this afternoon. He didn't find any reason to think he's faking. I mean, he—well, he said all the right things."

Of course he would. But I didn't say that. Instead, I said, "That's good."

She nodded, and her beautiful golden hair shimmered. "There's something else."

"What is it?"

"Well, I guess it's about us."

"You mean like the fact that we've been dating since Christmas?"

"Yes." She was looking at the ground and biting her lip.

I realized I was going to have to help her. I mean, one of the things I've always liked about Nicole is the fact that she cares about other people. Even though she'd been a little hard on me recently, she was normally very thoughtful. Right now she was worried about me. I said, "I think what you want to say is that Charlie has asked you out."

She looked up at me, and there were tears in her eyes. "Oh, Glen," she said. "I'm so confused. I really don't know what to do."

"Well, it's not as if we're going steady."

"Charlie said you told him to ask me out."

"I told him it was okay for him to ask you."

"So you don't mind if I go out with him?"

I remembered what Pastor Grant had said. "I want what's best for you."

"And you think I should go out with Charlie?"

I shrugged, "You know as well as I do the difference between me and Charlie."

Tears shone in her eyes. "It was you I always wanted to go out with. I've liked you ever since we moved here. You were so quiet and so—I don't know—almost bashful. You didn't seem to be interested in any girls. You were a bit like a mystery. For a long time, I wanted to get to know you and have you interested in me. Only—"

"Only once you got to know me, you discovered there was no mystery."

She responded quickly. "Oh, no. It's not that. It's just—I don't really know. Some things aren't the way I thought—"

I picked my words carefully. "But it's mainly about Charlie. You've changed your mind about wanting to go out with him now that he's accepted Christ."

"Glen, I was so sure I didn't like Charlie! To go with, I mean. He acted so smooth and he was so certain that he had all the answers that I just, well, I wanted to show him that he couldn't always get his way. Only—"

"Only you like him in spite of yourself," I supplied.

"I don't actually know if I like him or if I just feel sorry for him. He seems to genuinely regret the way he acted, and he's almost—almost shy. I don't want to hurt him. But I don't know if that means I like him. It's all mixed up in my mind."

"Yeah," I said, looking towards the church. "It's okay."

"Oh, Glen, I—"

"Don't worry about it. It's no big deal."

There were tears in her eyes, and I wanted to wipe them away. Instead, I moved so I was sideways to her. There were a few tears in my own eyes that I didn't want her to see.

"Is that all you wanted to say?" I asked brusquely.

"I guess. There isn't much to say, is there? I'm sorry about all the misunderstandings over Marta. I can't believe I acted so childishly."

"It's all part of growing up, I guess. Learning how to act." I paused, not sure if I should say what had come to my head. "By the way, Marta thinks you dislike her."

She didn't sound surprised. "Does she? I don't know if I would say I dislike her. But she's—well, she's not much like me, is she? I mean, we don't have anything in common. I don't know her very well. To be honest, I've never wanted to."

"No."

"I guess you must be disappointed in me. First Phil and now Marta—"

"Well, it's just that—I guess it's easy to judge people by what you know, even when you don't know much." I told her how I'd misjudged the vet at first. "I guess the truth is you have to get to know people beyond the surface before you try to figure out what they're like."

She picked up on my words. "And despite having gone to school together all those years, you and I really didn't know each other at all, either. Is that what you mean?"

It wasn't, but I had to admit it was true.

"I guess we both need to be more careful in the future."

"I don't want to see you get hurt," I said carefully.

"If you mean Charlie might hurt me, I know that's possible. But all I'll agree to is one date, and not right away, either."

"Yeah—well, take care."

"I will." She sighed. "I wish I could do something. I know what everybody will think."

I knew, too. But I'd live through it.

I led the way to the door of her house. I said, "Good-night," and turned to leave. But she didn't go in right away, so I put my arm around her waist and kissed her.

It was the first time I'd ever kissed a girl (not counting Marta who I hadn't really kissed) so it wasn't a particularly wonderful kiss. In fact, I barely realized what I was doing.

Nicole put her arms around me for a moment. She said "Good-night, Glen." Her voice was husky. "I'll see you at school." She went inside.

I leaned on the nearest wall for a minute. My head hurt. Nicole and I had broken up. Oh, yeah, she was just thinking about going on one date with Charlie. But knowing Charlie, anything could happen.

And the only satisfaction I had was that I had let her have the freedom to make her own decision.

Okay, to be honest, I'd known this day was coming ever since Charlie got back from Christmas holidays. Maybe even since the first night we went out together. That's why it had always seemed like a fairy tale.

Well, the fairy tale had ended, and what was left? A couple of souvenirs, a few memories, some bruises—what was that old saying? "Better to have loved and lost than never to have loved at all?" I'd heard that someplace recently and thought of Nicole and me. I wondered if it was true.

I walked to the car and started driving. After a few minutes, I realized I was headed toward the hospital. When I got there, I ducked past a nurse and hurried into Phil's room. He was alone, watching a dumb cop show on the TV that was set high above his bed. He looked over. "How did you get in?" he asked in surprise. "Isn't it a little late for visiting hours?"

"I know." I twirled an invisible cape. "But I have become a master of disguise."

He laughed.

It was the first time I'd heard him laugh since the accident.

"I don't think anyone spotted me," I said as I sat on the chair beside his bed. We talked for a while.

I guess I was kind of hyper. I was fighting the feeling of emptiness that I had felt from the moment Charlie had requested my permission to ask Nicole out. But I didn't say anything about it to Phil. I figured he had enough troubles of his own.

After about twenty minutes, a no-nonsense nurse came in and kicked me out.

I went, of course, but Phil grinned at me before I left, and I knew I'd been right to sneak in.

The funny thing was that as I left I realized I felt good. It was strange to know that even though Charlie had won, I could still feel okay about myself. Hey, I even felt good about his beating me up! Well, good that when it came right down to it, I had been able to take it.

I knew it would be a long, long time before I would be able to look at Nicole without feeling pain. But just because she was dumping me for Charlie didn't mean I had to go back into my shell and watch life pass by. There were others who needed me—like Phil and—who knew?—maybe even Marta.

Tears stung my eyes. Some of them were because of Nicole, but some were tears of joy. I guess I had known it in my head, but all of a sudden I had this overwhelming feeling that no matter how bad things seem to be, God loves me!

Long ago, he saw me fumbling away by myself and loved me, and he would no more abandon me than Mom and Dad would.

I don't remember ever in my life feeling this way before, but as I drove down the street, my whole body tingled with excitement. I was so overwhelmed by what God had done for me that I finally had to stop and park. After a few minutes, I dried my face with my sleeve. Self-consciously, I looked around, but I didn't see anyone.

I started driving again. My mind was all mixed up with thoughts of Christ and David, and of Nicole and Charlie and Phil, but out of the mess one thing came clear. My world was not going to end if Nicole wasn't meant for me. It didn't matter that Charlie had used me time and time again—even in accepting Christ so he could go out with Nicole. It didn't matter that Phil thought I was crazy to believe in God. It didn't even matter that all the kids might laugh at me behind my back when they found out Nicole had dumped me for Charlie. Because I'd finally realized who I was—I was Glen Sauten, and God made me just the way I am because he knows best.

So what if I never did all the things David had done? Frankly, I hoped I'd never have to do most of them. But there was one thing he'd done that I could do, and that was to be a "man after God's own heart."

Suddenly I knew what I was going to do in the fall! I was going to go some place where I could learn more about God and the Bible. I wanted to know enough so I could help other people the way Pastor Grant and John had helped me. Hey, there must be tons of Glen Sautens out there! Just ordinary people who needed to know there was a God who cared about them. And I had to learn how to tell them! And how to tell all the Phil Trents and the Marta Billings, too.

I didn't have a clue what my parents would think. But although they might be pretty puzzled, I knew they loved me, and they'd try to understand.

But what about the next six months before I could get away to college? What would happen with Charlie and Nicole? And Phil? And Marta? Not to mention Joyce. Nicole had said Joyce was too smart to get hurt. But was she? How would she feel when Nicole started going with Charlie? I realized I didn't know anything about Joyce, either. I'd never cared to know before. And old Mr. Smithers, and Pete and Colleen—there might be something I could do for them, too. Maybe even grumpy old Mr. Jackman. Would he be even harder to get along with after his son died? How could I begin to show him that he mattered to me?

I laughed. It sure must be God working in me, because I never would have thought like this on my own.

I parked the car and opened the kitchen door. There was a loud bark followed by a skittering sound across the linoleum. Scruffy was sliding toward me on his seat, not using his broken leg, but propelling himself across the floor as fast as he could with his little front paws.

I leaned over to rub him under the chin, and that silly little tail started thumping. I picked him up and he began licking my hand as if it was an all-day dog sucker.

I remembered that awful day I'd found him, and how scared and cold I'd been as I carried him along the road, and how John's truck had suddenly appeared after I prayed. Yeah, God was looking after me all right.

# Best of Friends

**by N. J. Lindquist**

**Glen Sauten:**

He thinks his parents baby him a bit too much, but generally life is pretty happy for Glen, although uneventful. Until he meets...

**Charlie Thornton:**

The new kid in town. Charlie has everything money can buy, including a shiny, red Mustang. Furthermore, his sophistication, athletic ability, and drop-dead good looks seem to attract every girl in school except...

**Nicole Grant:**

The pastor's daughter. Nicole is as beautiful as she is intelligent and remains unmoved by Charlie's advances—much to his frustration. And the amusement of...

**Phil Trent:**

Glen's best friend since kindergarten. But he is not amused to see Charlie take his place as Glen's new best friend, football quarterback, and the number one choice of every girl in town except Nicole.

Being Charlie's friend is not always easy for Glen. And keeping harmony between Charlie and Glen's other best friend, Phil Trent, is next to impossible. But it does lead to adventures. Countless adventures. In fact, Glen's whole life seems rocked by new experiences. Some of them life-threatening. And some life-changing!

## *Growing Up, Taking Hold...*

# In Time of Trouble

**by N. J. Lindquist**

**Shane:**
Everything he does seems to work out wrong. He's failing his classes, about to be fired from his part-time job, and barely speaking to his parents. Then there's the real problem—his twin brother...

**Sandy:**
Everything he does seems to be right. He's a star athlete, student president, and parents' dream child, with top marks, a great future, and many good friends. He'd never hang out with someone like...

**Marietta:**
A real looker, she's been Shane's girl-friend, but since Shane's dad took away his car, she's been unhappy. Maybe Shane should take a second look at...

**Janice:**
She's coming after Shane like a magnet to a fridge door. But is something fishy here? Just ask...

**Ernie:**
He's a loner who claims to be Shane's only real friend. But will he hang in when the real trouble hits?

What do you do when everything blows up in your face and you can't even trust your friends and family? How do you decide what you really want? Most important, how do you learn to trust yourself?

**If you have difficulty getting our books through your local bookstore, you can order from:**

**That's Life! Communications**

Box 487, Markham, ON L3P 3R1

Call tollfree 1-877-THATSLI(FE)
(In Toronto area (905) 471-1447)

email: thats-life@home.com

http://members.home.net/thats-life

*please print*

Quantity | | | Total
---|---|---|---
___ | **In Time of Trouble** | $6.95 US ($9.95 Canadian) | _______
___ | **Best of Friends** | $7.95 US ($9.95 Canadian) | _______
___ | **Friends Like These** | $7.95 US ($9.95 Canadian) | _______

___ Put me on your **mailing list** for new releases

Shipping & handling

1 book $3.00
2-6 books $6.00
7-10 books $9.00
11+ books 10% of total

In Canada, GST (7%) _______

Shipping costs _______

Total _______

Name: ______________________________

Address: ______________________________
apt. street

______________________________ | ______________
town prov./state code/zip

email: ______________________________

Excerpt from **In Time Of Trouble**

"Shane, you're late." Mr. Kaufmann was standing in the office doorway when I walked into the warehouse Friday after school. He had his hands on his hips, and it didn't take a genius to know he wasn't happy.

"Yeah, I know I'm late. But—"

He turned his back on my explanation and walked into the office.

I started to follow, but he returned almost immediately.

"I was going to wait until tomorrow," he said, "but there's no point. Here's the money we owe you. You're fired."

He held out an envelope, but I didn't take it.

"I said you're fired," Mr. Kaufmann repeated. "The only reason I've kept you on this long is that you worked well last summer when you were here full time. But since school started and you've been part-time—well, it just hasn't worked out."

"I don't get it. You're firing me because I was late today? I can explain that."

"It isn't today. It's your attitude. You do the least you can get away with. You really don't care if you do a good job or not. And some of the new kids are copying you. I can't have that. So here's your money."

He held the envelope in front of my face and this time I took it. But I felt more like stuffing it down his throat. What was to care about in moving boxes and loading trucks? I'd been doing the job, hadn't I? Spending every day after school and all day Saturday in this stinking place!

He went into the office and shut the door, so there was nothing for me to do but leave.

I knew the others were watching. Well, I didn't owe them anything. They were no friends of mine—just people I worked with.

I swore under my breath and walked back the way I'd come, grabbing my jacket off the hook as I went by.

And then I noticed the small tear on the sleeve.

How had that happened? Last night when I'd put my car in the shed and had brushed against the wall? I'd bought the jacket, an expensive black leather one, in the after-Christmas sale only a couple of weeks ago. Because of all the repairs to my car, and other expenses, the jacket had taken the last of my money. Now the jacket was already torn and the pay packet I was holding contained all the money I had left after working my butt off all summer and fall!

Anger surged through me. There was a stack of boxes near the doorway. I kicked them over, feeling a small amount of satisfaction when one of them opened and a bunch of small ball bearings went rolling all over the floor. I yanked open the side door and slammed it behind me as hard as I could.

The January cold cooled me off fast. I stopped to put on the jacket.

This was all my dad's fault! Just because I'd had another speeding ticket, he'd taken the keys to my car and told me I couldn't have them back for two weeks. And because I'd had to walk to work, I was late. So I was out of a job and it was all his fault.

I decided to go over to Ted's apartment and see if he was alone. Ted and I had been hanging around together a lot since last summer. He's a bit like me—eighteen and tired of being treated like a little kid. But we look kind of funny together. I'm blond, six-two, fairly muscular, and, they say, good-looking. Ted's short, maybe five-seven, and skinny—about a hundred and thirty pounds dripping wet. He has long, brown hair and a thin face with sharp features. Not exactly the guy you'd introduce to your favorite sister.

Our backgrounds are different, too. I've got a dad who's worked for the same company since he was my age, a mom who works part-time at the library, and a twin brother, Sandy. Ted lives in an apartment with only his father, who's had a ton of jobs and right now is a salesman for a men's clothing manufacturer. That means he travels a lot, which means Ted gets left alone a lot, which he likes.

Ted's kind of strange. His marks in school are terrible, but his street smarts would put him at the top of the class. He thinks life should be one big party, but, despite his size, he can defend himself pretty well when he has to.

His apartment is on the top floor of a four-story building. It's nothing to write home about, but it serves its purpose. Neither Ted nor his dad are what you'd call fussy.

When I got up to his door, I knocked, and I heard him yell, "Who is it?"

"Shane."

I heard him pulling back bolts. Then the door opened.

"Your dad here?" I asked.

"Naw, it's okay. I thought you worked today."

"No."

"Must have heard wrong."

Time enough to enlighten him later.

We spent several hours watching a movie he'd borrowed and drinking a few beers. Then we sent out for pizza. Stupid on my part because I should have saved what money I had left. Also stupid because if I didn't go home for supper my dad would be mad.

But sometimes it's easier not to face things. And this was one of those times.

So we ate pizza, had a couple more beers, and watched TV until suddenly Ted commented that it was eight o'clock.

Reality intruded. I jumped. "I'm supposed to pick up Marietta!"

"How?"

I stared at him. "What do you mean—how?" Then I remembered I had no car. And I hadn't arranged for a ride. I sat down.

"Get a ride with somebody."

"Yeah." I phoned a couple of kids and finally got somebody who'd pick me up and drive me to Marietta's. Ted came, too.

There was a party at Scott's house. Scott is another friend—well, sort of a friend. His parents are away a lot, so Scott has parties at his house frequently. I don't know if his parents are so stupid they can't tell, or if they just don't care.

Anyway, they never get in his way, so he keeps on having parties.

And that's where I was taking Marietta, the girl I had been going out with since last September. She's really something. Hard to believe she'd actually been going with me that long. That's a lot longer than she usually gives one guy.

She wasn't too pleased when she came to the door of her house. "You're late." She sounded a lot like Mr. Kaufmann.